SANTA LOVES CURVES

A BBW CHRISTMAS ROMANCE COLLECTION

LANA LOVE

LOVE HEART BOOKS

Also by Lana Love

For a full listing of my books, please visit:

https://www.loveheartbooks.com

❀ Created with Vellum

OH! OH! OH! SANTA

CHAPTER 1

TRISTA

I look in the full-length mirror and shake my head at my reflection. Is this what my life has really come to? If I wasn't so desperate for the money, I think I might be able to laugh at the red and white striped stockings, the acid-green dress, and the red and white hat. The dress is form-fitting, but it hides my swelling belly. It also helps that I'm overweight, because that means people look at me less.

"I don't know why *I* have to be Mrs. Claus." One of the other girls whines about her role for the mall's Santaland. "I mean, look at me! Obviously, I should be one of the elves, not going around wearing a totally unsexy fat suit."

I turn and try to ignore her. I'm not even sure if she knows that I'm in the dressing room. The girls she's with all laugh, making me wish I could just disappear. If it wasn't for the baby, I absolutely would not be here.

"Let's get going. You know that Mr. Moore gets totally pissy if we're not out there in time," another girl says. I watch her through the reflection in the mirror, and see her hiking up her skirt so that it's higher and she can show off more of her long, skinny legs. I wish my skirt was longer, but there's nothing I can do. I actually wouldn't mind being Mrs. Claus, but I'm here for the money, not a particular character.

"Do you think we're ever going to find out who Santa is?" Sally asks as she adjusts her skirt to show a little more leg. "He's got such a great voice. Like I'm totally sure it's familiar, but I can't figure out how or why."

"Girl, you think anyone you're interested in sounds familiar. You're as bad as some guys. *Hey bae, I know I know you, because I could never forget you.*"

I watch as they both erupt into laughter at what I assume must be an inside joke.

We walk out to Santaland and I can't help but grin like a kid. I've always loved Christmas more than anything in the world and the amount of happiness I feel at being one of Santa's elves makes this job so worth it. I love the carols and I love the little kids coming to tell Santa what they hope to get for Christmas. If I could, I'd buy each kid all of the gifts that they hope for. Every child should have their wishes come true at Christmas.

"Why don't you help me today?" I turn and see Santa Claus smiling at me, and my heart jumps a little bit when I hear his voice. They would make fun of me if I told them, but I agree with Sally – I recognize his voice, too, but I can't quite place it. I've wondered if he's an actor who's done local TV commercials. I don't have a DVR, so I always have to sit through the commercials if I want to watch anything on TV.

"I... I'm supposed to take wishes from the children?" Through the fake mustache and beard, I see Santa Claus smile at me and he is clearly amused. When he reaches out and grabs my hand and leads me to where he sits in Santa's chair, I melt and I can't disagree. One of the girls gives me a dirty look, but Santa Claus tells her to go do what I was going to do.

I'm not sure whether to be flattered or not. I do know that Sally is likely to tell me off later, for taking her job. But there's something about Santa Claus' smile that I can't resist. And maybe if I hear him talk a little bit more, I'll figure out why I recognize his voice.

I watch as all of the little kids line up - big, hopeful smiles on their little faces - their hands clutching their wish lists.

"One day, one of those kids will be mine." I put my hand on my stomach, feeling the very slight baby bump that I won't be able to hide much longer.

It's because of this baby that I'm even here. Money is tight enough as it is for just me, that I don't know how I'm going to make it as a single mom. But giving up my baby wasn't even an option. I knew that I had to give this child a chance and I've never wanted anything more than to be married with children.

Only thing, I don't know who the father is. Or rather, I do know who the father is, but I only ever got his first name. His name was Eddie, but I feel embarrassed that that's all I know. It's such a cliché, but we met one Saturday night when I was out dancing with some friends and I got a little drunk. I felt frustrated about still being a virgin, and the combination of how he danced with me and the cocktails I had, I went home – or rather to his hotel room – with him without a second thought. It felt so natural and fun, that I felt a little silly for having waited so long.

3

But then I freaked out and left before he woke up, and I figured it was just a random hookup him for him. Someone as sexy as he was would never like a girl like me, anyway. I was just the cute fat chick he took home that night, just for fun. Guys like him don't pursue girls like me.

"Earth to Trista," Santa Claus says, his bushy mustache and beard not hiding the big smile on his lips. "It is Trista, right? I like to know who my main elf is."

"Oh! Yes, Trista. It's Trista." The words splutter out of my mouth and embarrassments covers me like a wet blanket. "Sorry. I just get caught up in the season. I love seeing the kids," I say, trying to cover my real feelings. I love the kids, but I feel like I'm going to be giving my baby less than I want to be able to, because it's just going to be me. I think women who can manage being a single mom are amazing, it's just that I've always wanted to share raising a child with someone that I love.

"Good. I just wanted to make sure that you aren't going to run out on me."

Is Santa flirting with me?

"Oh, no. You're stuck with me, at least for today." I try and keep the tone of my voice light, but even I hear how my attempt at a joke falls flat.

"There's no other elf that I'd rather be stuck with. Now bring over the first kid." Santa pauses and clearly winks at me, and my knees wobble. "Unless you want to sit on my lap, instead? Would you like a taste of my candy cane?"

A kid screams somewhere in the mall, one of those high-pitched wails that sound like an air-raid siren, but Santa doesn't flinch or break eye contact with me.

I blink quickly, then usher the first kid over to Santa. I need to clear my thoughts, because everything I'm thinking and feeling right now is so deeply inappropriate.

The thing is, I do want to sit on Santa's lap and I want to ride his candy cane. And I have no idea who this man is!

CHAPTER 2

EDDIE

I watch my main elf and it's a good thing this Santa coat is oversize, because I'm hard as a goddamn rock. She keeps trying to pull the hem of her skirt down, but every time she bends over even slightly when she talks to one of the kids, the back of her skirt slides up and when I'm lucky, I catch a glimpse of her ripe, curvy-as-fuck ass.

I want to see that ass jiggle around, again, as I take her hard and fast. I'll show Santa doesn't come just once a year. How can she not remember even my *voice*? Well, okay, sure. We spent more time fucking than talking, but it's not like I didn't *try* to be a gentleman. *Fuck, man. Get it together.*

Having a raging boner when a kid sits on your lap is a one-way ticket to prison. I envision every sad thing I've ever endured, including the idea that this hot and sexy elf won't want to talk to me when she learns who I am.

"Here you go," she mumbles, handing me the card with the kid's wish list. I glance at it and my suspicions are confirmed

– it's nearly the same list I've seen from most other little boys that have come for their photo. Video games.

"Come here, little Tom."

"I'm not little!" Tom pouts at me as if I've gravely insulted him.

"Ho ho ho! Of course! You're a big, strong man!" I joke, really getting into my role. The rest of the guys in the band would have a field day with this, if they understood how much I'm starting to enjoy this gig. "Now tell Santa what you want for Christmas, and then let's smile for the camera."

Little Tom jumps on my lap and speaks faster than a disc jockey on speed, listing off the video games from his list, plus dozens more.

"Come here, Trista. You should be in this picture, too." I reach my gloved hand out to her. The blush on her face is a potent aphrodisiac. Sexy Elf will be mine.

I'm almost certain that Christmas is coming early this year. My manager had to talk me into this Santa gig, and now I want to give him a bonus.

Connor said it would be a good PR stunt for me to anonymously dress up as Santa and then fill kids' wishes for Christmas. I want kids of my own, but I thought it sounded like a total waste of time. Then I saw Sexy Elf. The moment I saw her was the moment that I found I would do this every year for the rest of my life if it means she can be my Mrs. Claus forever.

She obviously doesn't recognize me, though I don't know that anyone could, given this get-up that I'm dressed in. And we didn't exactly do much talking the first time we met, so it's not surprising that she hasn't recognized my voice. What is strange and a blow to my ego, is that she obviously doesn't know my music, because if she did, she would definitely recognize my voice.

"Aren't you going to give me presents?" Little Tom suddenly demands. His mother looks horrified and tries to pull him away, but Tom starts screaming.

"Hey, Tom. It's okay." I didn't even see Sexy Elf move, but suddenly she's on her knees in front of the boy, talking in a low voice. She says something I can't hear to the boy, then I watch as he nods and puts his hand in hers. She gently shakes his hand and whispers something in his ear that makes him smile.

I watch as Tom and his mother walk away, amazed at what I've just seen. The other elves are looking at Tom and his mother, their fake smiles not hiding the horror of what they've just witnessed with Little Tom.

"You were amazing just now," I tell Sexy Elf when she brings the next child, a girl with bright red and curly hair. Sexy Elf just smiles and looks away, but I can see a blush creeping across her cheeks. The little girl whose hand I'm holding jumps on my knee and starts in on her list of Christmas wishes while I'm still staring at Sexy Elf.

Sexy Elf is going to be the mother of my children.

THE DAY and the line of kids both go faster than I expect. I've always assumed that one day I would have a bunch of kids, but it's not something I've dwelled on since I hit it big. But today? Finding Sexy Elf and being around these kids unleashes a fierce need in me to build a family. Soon. It's suddenly the most important thing in the world.

"I..." Sexy Elf stutters as she faces me, her big eyes looking everywhere except at my face. "I guess I'll see you tomorrow?"

I don't want to wait until tomorrow to see her again, but I know I have to. One of the buttons of her costume has come undone, and her delicious tits are pushed up and on display, but she doesn't realize it. I want to lose myself in her creamy curves and make her the mother of my children. I'll buy a tour bus just for her and me, so that we never have to be apart and we can still have privacy.

"I'll walk back with you."

"Um, okay. I guess." Despite being nervous, I see a shy smile on her lips and I know she's mine.

The other elves try to get my attention, striking suggestive poses that leave no doubt about the kind of gift they want and will give more than willingly. They are pretty, but they have nothing on Sexy Elf. I walk a step behind her as we head to the dressing rooms, my eyes never leaving her curvy legs and the swish of her healthy hips. *Damn, I could get lost in that ass.*

"Um... I guess I'll see you tomorrow?"

Sexy Elf opens the door to the dressing room she shares with the other elves. She's not getting away that easily.

"No, you need to come with me. Now." I grab her by the arm and direct her to my dressing room. There's a look of surprise on her face, but she doesn't resist. My cock throbs from just touching her arm. Closing the door to my dressing room and locking it, I turn the and smile at Sexy Elf. "I've been wanting to do this since I saw you again."

"Again?"

Before she can say anything more, I close the distance between us in two steps, and then take her in my arms and claim her mouth with mine. She tastes sweet, like a candy cane, but I have a candy cane that I want her to taste.

Sexy Elf presses her body against mine and my cock aches from how badly I want to bury myself in her. They need to have her naked beneath me, her tits trembling as I take her over and over again, making her screaming my name.

I shove my knee between her legs and she doesn't resist. Grinding my cock against her, I groan as I feel the heat from her pussy. I reach under her skirt and pull down her crazy, striped tights and slide my fingers against her hot skin. They quickly find her slick pussy and I waste no time teasing at her clit and sliding my fingers inside her hot hole.

"Oh my God," she whispers in a hot exhale of breath. Her head tilts back and her eyes close, and I watch how she's letting her pleasure take over her body and how she's succumbing to it completely. She grinds down on my fingers and I can feel her body already shaking.

Sexy Elf wraps her arms around me and raises her mouth up to mine, begging for a kiss. I take her mouth again, invading it and massaging her tongue with my own. I lick and suck at her tongue as if it was my tongue on her clit instead of my fingers. She kisses me back with a pure abandon that deepens my desire for her.

There is no way I'm never letting her out of my sight again. She wiggles her hips and presses down, hard, on my fingers. I start kissing her so that I can watch her face, watch how beautiful she is when she comes.

"Yes, please! Yes! Just like that!" Her gorgeous blue eyes fly open and she stares deep into my eyes as her body bucks and presses on my fingers as her orgasm unleashes. Her pussy clenches my fingers and I want nothing more than to bury my cock deep inside of her and feel her pussy wrapped around my cock, milking me and planting my seed and babies in her belly.

"You are a fucking goddess when you come. You are beyond beautiful."

Sexy Elf's eyes are bright and her face is flushed beautifully from her orgasm. She looks at me and then something inexplicably shifts in her bright blue eyes. There's a look of alarm and it freaks me the fuck out.

"I… That was… It was amazing. But I've gotta go!"

CHAPTER 3

TRISTA

*O*h, look at Trista running! I bet she made a pass at Santa and he turned her down."

"Of course he did! Why would Santa choose a chunky girl when he could have one of us?"

Anger erupts inside of me, but I rush to our cramped dressing room and grab my things, before running out the door. I have to ignore the mean girls right now because I can't run the chance Santa coming out and finding me.

Everybody smiles and waves at me as I speed walk through the mall. I plaster a smile on my face, pretending to be happy, but my heart and mind are in such turmoil, being around other people right now is pure agony. *I wish I didn't need this job so bad, or I would just quit right now.*

When I finally make it out to the parking lot and my car, I breathe a huge sigh of relief. I sit in my car and hit the steering wheel. What am I going to do? My hand instinctively goes to my stomach and I rub the tiny bump. I love my baby with a blinding intensity that scares me, and we haven't even met yet. Being a single mom is going to be hard enough. Even if I wanted to, and I do want to, I can't be in a relationship right now.

What man is going to step up when I'm pregnant with another man's baby?

"Oh, hi. How are you Mrs. Nelson?" I close and lock my little mailbox, stuffing the bills deep in my purse.

"Trista, sweetheart. I've been meaning to find you."

The moment Mrs. Nelson calls me *sweetheart*, I know something is wrong. She's a cranky old lady at the best of times and she's only ever nice when she wants something.

"Oh, is there something I can help you with, Mrs. Nelson?" I cross my fingers because I'm pretty sure I know what's coming.

"Well, not per se." The tone of her voice changes slightly, like she's talking to someone beneath her. "I wanted to let you know that rent is going up in two months. I know you're… on a limited budget, so I wanted to let you know in case you need to find other living arrangements. I'll put a formal letter in your mailbox in the next day or two, but I just wanted to let you know."

My heart sinks like a stone and I feel dizzy when the blood drains from my face. This is terrible news.

"Thanks for letting me know. I'm sure everything will work out fine." I smile at Mrs. Nelson and then turn down the hallway to my apartment.

When I get into my apartment, I collapse on the couch and start to cry. How will I make it through this? I'm barely out of college and I don't have a great job, and I have a baby on the way. I've been determined that I can do all of this on my own, but a voice in my head says that letting myself go that one night and having a one-night stand was a monumental mistake.

I hadn't seen my friend Pauline in months, and she insisted on going out to a club and dancing all night. But then I met this man who dances better than any man I've ever seen before. In the close confines of the club, we pressed our bodies against each other and he moved his hips against mine in a rhythm that made me weak. When he whispered into my ear that we should go back to his place, I let my hormones take over and I said yes.

That man, a stranger, is the only man I've ever slept with. We barely exchanged first names, and I have no idea how to contact him. He was handsome and charming, and it was the best night of my life. But now I feel I'm being punished for a mistake, by having life throw one curveball at me after the next. I know I can figure everything out, but this is just so much harder than I expected it to be.

I let myself get lost in the memories of the man that I danced and slept with. What would it be like to spend Christmas with him, every Christmas? Him and our baby, a loving little family. We would hold hands and go caroling, smiling at everyone, and pause for a kiss every time we found mistletoe. If there was snow, we would stop and make snow angels. Every minute of our lives would be the best Christmas gift, ever.

Having a family and husband of my own has always been my ultimate dream.

I just never thought I'd have the baby without the husband.

But what about Santa? I don't know what's coming over me that I'm just letting myself go when a man talks to me in just the right way. I haven't even seen the man's face, but there's something about him that is magnetic. It feels like he sees me and wants me for exactly who I am.

That can't be right, though. It's always the skinny girls who have this kind of thing happen – not the girls who have something extra like I do.

Yet it felt like there was something special with him. *Trista, stop fooling yourself. You just made it easy for him.*

I place my hands over my stomach and curl up on my couch. Determined not to lose myself in sadness, I turn on Netflix and watch sappy Christmas movies. They're always a little bit cheesy and so predictable, but also comforting and fun.

I want a movie-worthy romance for Christmas.

CHAPTER 4

EDDIE

*Y*o, Eddie. How's it hanging? How much longer you want to stay at the mall?"

I lean back in my seat as my driver takes me to the mall. Never in my life did I think I would be excited to go to a mall.

"I want to do the reveal today. I know it's early, but it's important. Can you arrange the media on short notice?"

Eddie inhales sharply and I know he's flipping me the bird. I also know that he can make the media happen.

"Fuck, man. What's gotten into you? You hate the mall that much?"

"Nah, Conor. It's turned out to be a pretty sweet gig. I found Mrs. Savage." I close my eyes as I think about Sexy Elf. The way her lips parted when she was coming and how erotic it was to make her come like that in my dressing room. I only know her first name, though I prefer to call her Sexy Elf, but I know she's going to be my wife.

"You what? The famously single Eddie Savage has found a wife? How on God's goddamn green earth did that happen?" Conor bellows with laughter and I can't blame him. I've slept with plenty of groupies and plenty of beautiful women, but I never let any of them stay around long enough for a relationship, because none of them were right. Sexy Elf is special and I know that she's the one, even though I don't know anything about her.

"It's hard to explain, Conor. But I'm dead certain about this. Look, the car's pulling into the mall now. Make it happen."

WHEN CONOR TOLD me about this gig, it wasn't exactly what I imagined when I told him that I wanted to do something in the community for Christmas. I thought he'd come up with something like visiting a school or a visit at a Children's Hospital. The idea of dressing up as Santa Claus wasn't exactly my first choice.

Now, the man deserves a raise. I've never stopped thinking about that one night with Sexy Elf and it's a stroke of unimaginable luck that I found her again.

"Here we go, boss." I adjust my beard and my hips and I step into the parking lot.

It's a welcome change to have kids screaming and running up to me than it is to have gold-digging groupies screaming at me. I camp it up with kids as I walk through the mall, shaking hands and posing for pictures. There is something pure and reassuring about is the absolute faith in Santa Claus that children have. The world can be harsh, but interacting with these kids makes me feel like a better man. Nothing can stop me from grinning as I approach Santa land in the mall.

Today, Sexy Elf is leaving with me.

"OH, can I be your assistant today?" One of the lesser elves coos at me. The way she's just throwing herself at me is so unappealing. It would work with any of the other men in my band, but not for me.

I only have eyes for Sexy Elf.

"I'm afraid that position is filled. By the way, have you seen Se... the girl who's been my assistant?" I ask, looking around the Santaland area.

"Not sure. She ran out of here yesterday like a social media outcast. I'm happy to fill in for her," the elf says, leaning over and giving me an up close and personal view of her tits.

"No, thank you," I say, struggling to keep control. If Sexy Elf isn't here, I'm going to leave and track her down. "Excuse me."

I stride as fast as I can, given this big red suit, which is to say not very fast. Another one of the elves tries to stop me, but I brush by her. There's only one elf I want to see and I won't stop until I find her. I barge into the dressing room and find Sexy Elf sitting in front of a mirror, her head resting in her hands.

"Hey," I say, a different kind of urgency filling me as I breathe a sigh of relief at finding her. "Why are you..."

I freeze when she looks at me, her eyes red and filled with tears. Before I can breathe another breath, I'm at her side and pulling her into my arms.

"It'll be okay. What's wrong?"

Sexy Elf pushes out of my arms and looks at me, her blue eyes wild. Her eyes dart around the small dressing room, as if looking for an escape.

"Why…" Her spectacular chest heaves as she catches her breath. "Why do you care?"

I step back, taken by surprise.

"Because I care about you."

"You mean that yesterday wasn't just some random thing, some random 'give the fat girl some attention' pity?"

"What? No!" Alarm bells ring in my head and I realize if I don't handle this properly, she's going to flee again – and this time she won't come back. Her eyes hold a fierce challenge as she stares at me and I have to know what's going on and why she's so upset. "I need to come clean."

Sexy Elf rolls her eyes and takes a more defensive posture. For the first time, I'm scared. Scared that she runs away from me and shuts me out completely. As much as I need her, I can't take her if she doesn't want to be with me.

"Have you ever wondered why none of you has seen me without my costume and beard?"

"Uh, yeah. It's all the other girls talk about. They think they recognize your voice and it's driving them crazy that they can't figure out who you are."

"What about you?" Sexy Elf takes a deep breath, her nervousness rolling off her in waves. "Pulling your dress isn't going to make it any longer, you know."

"I shouldn't have taken this job," Sexy Elf mutters, giving up on pulling at her dress.

"Yes, you should have. I'm ecstatic to have found you again."

Sexy Elf rolls her eyes and turns away and walks toward the door.

"Wait. You said again? That's the second time you've said that."

"I did. And you haven't answered my question about whether or not you recognize my voice. You first."

"Okay, fine." Sexy Elf turns back to me, rolling her eyes. "It does sound familiar, in a way. I don't obsess over it like the other girls are, though. Lots of people sound like other people."

"Maybe this will help you." I take off my beard and hat, and run my hand through my hair.

"Wow, you're hot!" Sexy Elf exclaims, then slaps her hand over her mouth. "Sorry," she mumbles.

"You're sexy when you don't censor your reactions." I grin as I watch a crimson blush color her face and chest. I love her even more, watching how she reacts to me – and we haven't even gotten to the really good stuff. Yet.

"Oh my God! It's you! From the club! We… um, I went home with you! Um, but sorry, I don't know who you are, other-wise. You said your name was Eddie, but should I know who you are?"

"You really are one in a million," I say, astounded to find the one woman on the planet who *doesn't* know who I am. "I'm Eddie Savage. And yes, I remember that night with you… exceptionally well. You were highly memorable."

"Who?" Sexy Elf looks at me, and I watch as her eyes shift from confusion to wonder. "You're… Whoa. You remember *me*?"

"Ah, so you haven't been living on Mars the last few years," I tease, happy that I can see a smile playing at the corners of her mouth. At least she's *heard* of me.

"You're the guy that sang *Endless Honey*, right? Oh my God. I… holy cow. The other girls will die when they find out!"

"Do you really not know anything about me?"

"Not really, no. I studied a lot in college and have been working a lot ever since. I don't really know current bands. Sorry."

"Don't be sorry," I say, going to her and pulling her into my arms, thrilled when she doesn't resist. I place a kiss on her lips, teasing her with the tip of my tongue. "You don't know how refreshing that is. Don't mention who I am, though. Not yet. They'll know by the end of today, but it's a special surprise for the kids."

"What?" Sexy Elf leans into me and having her in my arms makes me joyous.

"But I have something I need to tell you, too. It's really important."

"It can wait." The sound of the other elves in the hallway makes us step apart quickly. "Not a word," I say, putting my finger on her plump, sexy lips, lust raging in my body. "You'll see."

CHAPTER 5

TRISTA

*E*ddie puts his beard and hat back on, and I follow him out of the dressing room. The other girls stare at us, their mouths hanging open as we walk past them.

"What's going on?" I hear them whisper.

I'm just trying to wrap my head around that Eddie is the guy from the club. He's the father of my baby! Butterflies fill my stomach. What will he say when he finds out? He likes me now, but will he even believe me when I tell him the baby is his? I gave him my virginity that night, but I never told him that.

The beginning of the shift is like every other – kids excited and parents looking alternately stressed and happy, the same set of Christmas carols playing over the tinny sound system. The photographer looking like he's at the end of his patience.

Eddie keeps looking around, his eyes searching the crowd.

"Is everything okay?" I ask as one kid bounds back to their mom and one of the other elves takes the wish list from a new kid.

"Everything is perfect. You'll understand, soon."

"OH MY GOD! Do I look okay? Tell me my makeup hasn't melted off my face!"

I turn when I hear the other elves shrieking. There's a commotion outside of Santaland and lots of people are pointing as a camera crew and a bunch of people walk towards us.

"Um, the other elves are distracted. Do you want me to get the next kid?" I ask Eddie, who is grinning.

"No, not yet, sweetheart. This is why I wanted you to wait about telling anybody who I am."

Before I can say anything else, he's walking toward a very well-dressed man who has one of the reporters from the local news trailing behind him.

"Yo, Eddie, my man. Or should I say Santa?" And he laughs and they do that complicated handshake half-hug thing that guys do.

"Keep it Santa, for the kids."

"You got it. This here is Serena. She's going to interview you for the local news and break the story. A couple of national networks are on their way, but they're going to be playing catch-up to Serena."

Serena looks like a professional Barbie doll; her makeup and hair styling puts the other elf girls to shame. She's grinning with a megawatt smile and she flicks her pin-straight hair back with manicured fingers.

"It is *such* a pleasure to meet you Mr. Savage. If you would like to do a follow-up interview, later, I am completely at your disposal." I cringe when I hear how this woman is talking to Eddie. She would clearly do anything for him and give him anything he asked for, including her body.

"I'm sure this interview will be plenty. Now where do you need me to stand?"

"We need to get a couple of establishing shots, so let us get those, first. We'll need you sitting down, for that."

He walks back toward where I'm standing looking so happy, it makes me feel happy too, even though I have no idea what is going on.

"What is all this?" I whisper quickly.

"I'm doing a surprise giveaway. I'm granting all the Christmas wishes for all of the kids." Eddie says quickly.

He really is a good man. I always thought that rock stars were sex and drug-crazed lunatics, but Eddie just seems a normal guy.

I glance over to the other elves and they're looking at me with undisguised jealousy on their faces. When one of the people with Serena comes over to them and instructs them on where to stand, they all smile very nicely and arch their bodies in the direction of the camera.

"Give them your best smile," Eddie says, quickly reaching toward me and stroking one of his fingers along the edge of my hand. A different kind of happiness bubbles up inside of me. Could it be that he really likes me? He completely ignores the other elves and he politely shut down Serena.

But that seems way too much for me to wish for. I wouldn't even wish that in my wildest dreams, because rock stars don't like curvy girls like me.

"Okay. We got the shots. Now," Serena says, her voice clear and authoritative, "I'm going to do an intro, so please everybody keep quiet. After the intro, I'll interview Eddie Savage. Or, as everyone here has known him, Santa Claus."

Serena goes and stands in front of two cameras and says something to the cameramen. Some bright lights, and they make me squint, then Serena starts talking. I do my best to remember to smile.

"I'm Serena Maloney, coming to you from Fairpoint Mall. Today, I'm pleased to break a heartwarming story that will fill you with Christmas spirit. After working here this week undercover, rock megastar Eddie Savage will be granting all of the wishes of all the children who have sat on his lap and shared their Christmas wish lists. Now, let's talk with Santa." After a long pause, Serena says "cut" and then she walks over toward Eddie and me.

"Okay, now you can move to the side. We don't need you in this shot," she says to me. The smile on her face doesn't reach her eyes and I can hear the veiled Mean Girl threat behind it. As soon as I start to move away, Eddie reaches out and grabs my hand in his.

"No, she stays. She's with me." Eddie's voice is firm, his hand not letting go of mine.

"No, it's okay," I say, shy about even the thought of being on the local news, much less national news.

"Please, stay." The look in Eddie's eyes is caring and his voice has an authority that tells me he means business.

Nerves race through me and I just nod my head.

"Well, this is… unexpected, but we can work with it. Honey," Serena says, giving me her fake mega-watt smile, "just smile and try to look natural."

"Okay."

"And start rolling," Serena calls out to the cameramen. "Now tell us, Eddie – or should I call you Santa Claus?"

"Call me Santa, for the kids." Eddie smiles at Serena and tugs my hand so that I'm standing closer to him.

"Well, Santa, can you tell me what you're doing here? Shouldn't you be on tour?"

Eddie laughs and it unwinds some of the tension within me. Eddie squeezes my hand and it makes me feel special and like he's still thinking about me, despite being interviewed for television.

"We do have a new tour, but it doesn't start until the new year. I'm here because I want to give back to this community. We've been keeping track of all the wish lists of the kids who have come to visit me, and I'm pleased to say that I will be granting every wish from those kids, in addition to making a large donation to the local children's hospital. Every kid should have all of their wishes come true and I just want to help that happen."

"That's wonderful. How much longer will you be here, in case our viewers want to come and share their lists with you?"

"Well, Serena, today's my last day. However, I will be granting all the wishes that are delivered here, now through the end of the week."

"Oh, I'm sure that I'm not the only one that will be sorry to hear that. It's not often we have a musician such as yourself doing something like this for our community. Any chance you'll be staying longer?"

"Well," Eddie says, breaking his eyes away from Serena and looking at me. My insides go to liquid and my heart feels like it's going to burst out of my chest. "That depends on what Se… what my favorite elf here says."

CHAPTER 6

EDDIE

I catch myself just in time before I say Sexy Elf on television. Though, I should really call her Trista, which I do remember from when we met. That night we met and I took her back to my hotel, it's a night that I remember every single detail about.

"Trista, will you please come with me?"

Her eyes turn as big as saucers and excitement courses through my veins. I lead her over toward the side of Santa Land, where a big piece of mistletoe is hanging.

"Is that mistletoe?" She asks, looking up.

"You bet your sexy self it is," I whisper, then pull her into my arms and give her the biggest, most dramatic kiss I can manage. I bend her backwards and stroke her tongue with my own, my cock instantly hard as I feel her soft, luscious body pressed against mine.

Trista sighs in my arms and then yields to my kiss and returns it with passion. My body lights up like the Christmas tree we're standing next to and I know that there will never be another present that is better than Trista and this kiss. Well, not until she has my babies, that is.

"Trista, my darling elf," I say, looking into her bright eyes as she catches her breath, "will you be my wife? Will you be my Mrs. Claus until the end of time?"

Trista opens and closes her mouth, then gives me the prettiest smile I've ever seen.

"Yes! Oh my God, yes!"

She launches herself back into my arms and kisses me with an intensity that makes me stagger. This woman has so much depth, that I can't wait to spend the rest of my life with her.

"Now there's something I need to tell you," she whispers in my ear. "I'm pregnant with your baby. From that night."

"What?" I find my true love after I thought I lost her, and now she's telling me she's having our baby? This really is the best Christmas ever!

"It's true!" Trista says, her voice suddenly shy and quiet.

"You have made me the happiest man on earth, twice over!" I cover her face with kisses, ignoring Serena and everyone else here. Trista is the only person who matters.

"And there you have it, viewers! Eddie Savage is granting the Christmas wishes of children here in Fairpoint, and – you saw it here first – is now engaged!"

Serena cuts filming and I couldn't be happier. I want to go away with Trista, right this second, and nothing is going to stop me.

"If you'll excuse us," I say to her and the other elves. "I need to spend some time with my future wife."

CHAPTER 7

TRISTA

*a*s soon as Eddie takes off his beard and hat, women and girls in the mall start screaming. He grabs my hand, smiles wickedly, and then we take off running. I'm laughing and bubbling over with excitement, because this feels like a movie. It feels so unreal that a famous rock star even knows my name, much less wants anything to do with me.

"Do you have anything in the dressing room that you need?" Eddie asks, breathlessly, as we make it to the parking lot and are finally able to stop running.

"Oh, crap! My purse!" I look back toward the doors to the mall, and the thought of leaving Eddie right now makes me sad.

"Don't worry about it. I'll have my driver go pick it up. Now that I have you," he says, pulling me close to him and wrapping his arms around me, "I'm not letting you out of my sight for a single second."

"I think I like the sound of that," I say, pressing my body against his and enjoying this moment.

I watch as Eddie takes out his phone and listens as he gives his driver directions on where to go and what my purse looks like.

"Okay. He's going to pull the car around here so we can get in, and then he's going to go fetch your purse."

"What will we do in the meantime?" I tease, reaching up and running my fingers through Eddie's dark hair. He lowers his head, so that his lips just above mine and I can feel the air move when he speaks.

"I have a few ideas..." Eddie's lips meet mine and it feels like all of the Christmas lights are lighting up inside of me.

"WELCOME TO MY HUMBLE TEMPORARY ABODE." And he extends his arm in a grand gesture, motioning for me to walk into his palatial hotel suite.

"Oh my God! This is out of this world!" We walk further into the suite and my mouth literally drops open. The leather of the couch is more luxurious than anything I've seen, not to mention the view over the city and the artwork on the walls. This place looks fancier than something in the magazine.

"Get used to it, babe. This is your life from now on, if you want it."

I turn and look at Eddie, unsure if I've heard him correctly. But he's not joking and he's looking at me in a way that I've never had a man look at me — he looks genuine and caring and like he would move heaven and earth for me. My heart thumps wildly in my chest and I feel like I need to pinch myself to make sure I'm not dreaming.

"I... But what about." I look down and put my hand on my stomach. I barely even have a baby bump and you can't see it unless I'm naked.

The look in Eddie's eyes softens and he stares at my stomach.

"You're serious?" His eyes lift and meet mine, and their probing.

"I'm absolutely serious, Eddie. You're the only man I've ever slept with."

Eddie's mouth falls open and then he smiles so broadly that I think his face is going to crack.

"You are amazing, Trista. You've just given me everything that I've ever wanted — a stunning wife and a family. I love you."

"I love you, too!" I blurt the words out, and feel my cheeks burn with a blush. Waves of excitement and nerves jangle my body. Ever since Eddie revealed who he was to me, I've known that he was the one for me. That he is the only one for me.

Ever since that night that we spent together, I've never stopped thinking about him even though I only knew his first name, but we just clicked so well that night and the way he made my body feel was truly mind blowing. But I'd been so scared when I woke up, early in the morning, that I fled.

"Then come here and let me show you how much I love you."

I walk over to Eddie, watching as he pulls the Santa suit off of his body.

"Wait! What if I want to sit on Santa's lap?" I tease.

"Come here, my Sexy Elf," Eddie says, a deliciously wicked smile on his lips. "Santa *does* have a candy cane for you. Would you like to taste it?"

"Oh, yes, Santa. I want to taste your candy cane."

Eddie goes over to the couch, his Santa coat unbuttoned and falling open. I unbutton the top of my dress as I walk over to him, swinging my hips as I do.

When I'm standing in front of Eddie, he sits up and rips my dress off me. The cheap fabric falls to the floor and my hands instinctively try to cover up my stomach.

"No," Eddie says, his voice low and urgent. "I want to see you. All of you. You're fucking gorgeous!"

He puts his hands on mine and I let him move my hands. I relax when I see the lust and appreciation in his eyes.

"Your baby is in here," I say, putting his hand back on my stomach. "It's not kicking yet, but it will be soon enough."

I hate that I need to, but I need to see that he's really committed to me and our baby.

"I'm not going to stop touching you or your stomach, especially when my son – *our* son – starts kicking."

Relieved, I take a step closer so that my legs are pushing against the leather couch he's sitting on. I look down into his eyes, a warmth of love and desirability intoxicating me. Finding Eddie again is more than I ever imagined could happen. What were the odds?!

"Is there something I can help you with, Sexy Elf?" Eddie's green eyes flash wickedly as he puts his hand on my hips, pulling me closer to him.

"Maybe I want to sit on Santa's lap…" I tease, putting a finger in my mouth and sucking it slowly. "Is that allowed?"

Eddie rips apart the crotch of my striped elf tights, then gasps.

"Commando?"

"Laundry day."

"I think I love you even more, Sexy Elf! Now come to Santa."

Feeling more confident than I ever have, I straddle Eddie's lap and rub my wetness along the length of his massive cock. It bumps up against me and I bite my lip remembering how he filled me up so perfectly and felt so, so good inside of me.

"Finding you again is the best Christmas present, ever," I say, lowering my face to his and kissing him passionately. His tongue flicks at mine and it makes me squirm with anticipation.

"I feel lucky," Eddie says, running his hands over my skin and then cupping my ass, "to have found you, and my child." I gasp as he pushes into me, my body fitting tightly around his throbbing cock. "Fuck, you feel amazing. I found everything when I found you again."

Deep emotion rises within me and I lose myself in pleasure as I rock my body over Eddie's, and look deep into his eyes. I bounce on his cock, sometimes taking him shallowly, teasing him, and then quickly sliding down his full length and taking him deep inside of me. He fits inside of me so perfectly that I would be thrilled to spend the rest of my life doing just this, with him.

"Oh, wow!" I cry out when Eddie lifts one of my breasts to his mouth, and sucks ferociously, my nipple contracting so much that hurts as he massages his tongue against it. I wrap my arms around Eddie as little explosions go off in my body, my orgasm so close that my body is shaking like an earthquake about to blow. "I'm so close!"

Eddie moves his hips below me, stroking my g-spot as if his cock was made just for me. I cry out even more when he lowers his hand to my pussy and massages my clit with his thumb. Wetness gushes from me and I grind and wiggle on his cock, working to push both of us over the edge so that we can come at the same time.

"Fuck! You're amazing!" Eddie groans and his eyelids fall to half-mast, and he wraps his muscular arms around my body and pulls me so that we're chest to chest and our bodies are moving in perfect time together. His heartbeat thumps so hard I can feel it in my chest; it matches how strongly my heart is beating and how much my heart is overflowing with love for him. "Come with me, Trista!"

Our lips locked in a deep, probing kiss, my body takes over, thrashing above him as he thrusts up into me and we both come in unison. We moan into each other's mouths, and it's the most intimate thing I've ever experienced. He slams his massive cock deep inside of me and then holds me so that he stays deep inside of me.

My body explodes in pleasure and my body shakes as our bodies become one. Eddie's cock throbs and his body bucks as he comes, too. His breathing is hard and fast, and the look in his green eyes is passionate and wild.

I cover his face in kisses, feeling happier than I ever have before.

"I promise the next time I'll last longer, Trista. There's just something about you that makes me lose control and I can't contain myself when I'm with you."

I smile as I look at Eddie, a warm pride rising up in me that I can make him, such a powerful and successful man, lose control. Eddie makes me feel special and valuable, like I matter more than anything else in the world.

"Maybe I should take off these tights?" I laugh, looking down and seeing how the hole Eddie ripped is even larger now.

"Hmm. I think I'm going to have to make a habit of ripping your clothes off of you."

"I think they'll get expensive." I giggle as he traces his fingers over my sensitive skin.

"I'll buy you new lingerie every day of the year. Anything for my gorgeous and sexy wife." And he wraps his lips around one of my breasts, his tongue roughly flicking at my sensitive nipple.

I groan from deep inside of my body and how much pleasure Eddie is giving me. I tremble above him and my hips instinctively rub over his cock, inviting him for more.

"I love you so much, Eddie."

"I love you too, my Sexy Elf. Now let's see how long we can last this time."

EPILOGUE – TRISTA & EDDIE

This is my favorite time of year," I say, snuggling into Eddie as our car drives us to the mall. "I love that you played Santa again this year. We got so many emails and cards last year – it was such a special thing for all the children."

I slide my hand under Eddie's Santa coat and let my fingers slide against his muscular stomach. Eddie pushes into my hand and a giggle rises up in me. It's been a year since we came together, but every day still feels special and sparkly, like it did right at the beginning. Everything is magical with Eddie and I wouldn't trade it for the world.

"Wait until we're home," Eddie says, kissing my lips quickly as he puts his hand on mine and pulls it out from his jacket. "Jake has only just fallen asleep."

Eddie looks at our son and his eyes glaze over with unadulterated love. Jake huffs and snores lightly as he sleeps, and he looks like an absolute angel. His little fists move, grasping at the air in front of him. Despite all the nights of too little sleep and all the dirty diapers and how demanding a baby is,

I love our son with an infinite love and ferociousness I didn't know I was capable of.

"If you insist," I say, sticking out my lip in a pout. "Hey!" I start giggling when Eddie reaches down and pushes up my skirt and tickles the inside of my thigh. "What happened until waiting until we're home?"

Eddie's fingers move up the inside of my thigh and I stifle a moan as my body lights up with love and desire. He loves my body and all my curves more than even I do. He always leaves the lights on – demanding it – because he loves my body and how it moves when we make love.

I spread my legs in invitation, not wanting him to stop. I'm always completely blissed out because of how often we make love. We just can't get enough of each other.

"But we should wait until we get home," Eddie teases as he stills his fingers on my thigh. I sigh in frustration and bite my lip, and look at him. His green eyes have a wicked glint in them, and it makes me need him even more.

"You're evil, you know that, right?" I laugh as I move in my seat, clenching my thighs to try and take the edge off.

"Well, have you been naughty or nice this year, Trista? That's what Santa needs to know."

"I've been very good... at being naughty." I giggle, then run my tongue along his neck, and then nip at his earlobe in the way that makes him shiver. Eddie groans and I can feel his heart beating faster, underneath his Santa coat. When my hand goes down between his thighs, I feel how hard he is already. I stroke his hard cock, getting wetter as he pushes into my hand, asking for more. As soon as I hear him moan, I pull my hand back. "But you're right, Eddie. We should wait until we get home."

"Trista." There's a sexy danger in the tone of his voice and I know that I've pushed him to a point where he can't come back from.

"Is there something wrong?" I lick my lips and reach out and touch his cock again, and it jumps in my hand. "I think I know how to solve this, so that you're more... comfortable."

I click the button for the privacy window goes up and the driver can't see us.

"Please take the long way home," I ask over the intercom.

"Of course, Mrs. Rayford."

The intercom clicks off and I unbutton my blouse and unhook the front clasp of my bra, and then slide down onto my knees, between Eddie's legs.

"You are being very naughty," he says, his voice heavy.

I quickly undo the belt and zipper on his pants, then pull them so that his cock is free. I wrap my fingers around his thick, hard shaft.

"But you're not stopping me." I lower my head quickly and take the tip of his cock into my mouth, swirling my tongue around the tip and tasting his salty goodness. I lift my hand and look up at him as I lick my lips. "Would you like me to stop?"

"No," Eddie says, his voice heavy with need. "I need you to be naughty, Trista."

"But will I still get presents if I'm naughty?" I ask, with an exaggerated innocence. I stroke him more firmly now, twisting my fingers around head of his cock in just the way that I know he loves.

Eddie closes his eyes and tilts his head back, groaning. He pushes up into my fingers and his cock throbs in my hand.

"Trista, you will receive even better presents if you're naughty right now. But I want to watch you come, too."

"I can make that happen, too." I loosen the waistband of my skirt, and slide one of my hands underneath my tights and into my panties. My fingers find my hot slickness and I rub my clit as I wrap my lips around Eddie's cock.

"Fuck. That feels so good." And he runs his fingers through my hair and I look up and see him watching me. Jolts of pleasure overtake my body as I finger myself and I take more of Eddie, deep in my mouth so that he's hitting the back of my throat. I love the way he tastes and the way he's just a little too big for my mouth.

My heart races as I get closer to finishing and I work my mouth faster over his cock, feeling Eddie tremble in that way he does just before he's about to come. I slide my mouth off of his cock, and Eddie groans in agony. I wipe the spit and pre-cum, from my mouth, and then wrap my hand around his cock and pump him as I look up into his face.

"I want to watch you come, too," I gasp as my body trembles, on the edge of the orgasm. "I want you to come on my boobs."

And he groans even louder and his hips thrust up against my hands and then he explodes on my chest. That sends me over the edge too, and I bite my lip so that I don't cry out with my pleasure and wake Jake.

I rub his come over my breasts and stomach, and Eddie twitches as he watches me. I know he loves this and that I'm teasing him even more by touching myself like this.

"Come up," Eddie says, extending his hand to me and studying me as I move back up onto the bench seat. "You are so fucking amazing, Trista. You are a one-in-a-million woman."

"I think I know the lyrics to that song," I smile, love rushing through me as I remember his song that went platinum last year.

Before New Year's had even rolled around, Eddie wrote an entire album that he dedicated to me. It launched at number one, and *One in A Million Woman* was a smash, international hit, even bigger than *Endless Honey*. My body always shivers when I hear the song on the radio, because it still feels unreal that this song is about me. Curvy me. Who would've thought that I would win the heart of Eddie Savage?

But I'm glad I did. Eddie and Jake are my everything.

"I thought you might remember that song. I mean, the whole album is about you and how much I love you." Eddie pulls me close to him and kisses me long and slow. My body lights up like the Christmas lights we're passing and I can't wait to get home so that we can give Jake to the nanny, and then fall into bed and make love all night long.

"I love you, too, Eddie. I can't imagine life without you. You have made me the happiest woman and mother in the world. I wouldn't give up any of this for anything."

"And you have made me the happiest man and father in the world, Trista. My love for you will never end."

BEIGNETS AND MISTLETOE

CHAPTER 1

MARIAN

*W*ould you like to order dessert?" The waiter stands stiffly next to our table.

"I know it's evening, but do you have any beignets? I just love them so much!" I feel as excited as a little kid as I look up at the waiter. If you asked me last week if I'd fall in love with little fried squares of dough dusted in powdered sugar, I'd have laughed. Now, they're all I want to eat. That crispy dough, the powdery sweet of the sugar? They're perfect and they're just one of the things about New Orleans that I've come to love.

"Actually," my mom interrupts, "we have someone joining us. Please give us a few more minutes." My mother smiles very sweetly, but the commanding tone of her voice is clear and the waiter nods before he turns and walks away. She does not approve of my love of beignets.

"Mom, who's joining us?" I look from my her to Dad, a frustration bubbling up in me when neither of them answers my question.

"It's a surprise, sweetheart." I cringe at the way my mom says this. There's an air about her that sets alarm bells ringing, but this is a fancy restaurant and we're on a family vacation for Christmas, so I can't escape, no matter how much I want to.

"You know I don't like surprises…" I mean, I do like surprises, I just don't like surprises that my mom mastermists for me. They're always more about her than they are about me. She means well, but she still hasn't realized or accepted that I'm not a carbon copy of her.

"It's not right that you're still single – especially now that it's Christmas. It's such a lonely time to be on your own. When are you going to settle down?"

"Mom," I sigh, already tired from the inevitable argument. It's only the fifth time she's said this since we arrived in New Orleans for our Christmas vacation…and we arrived yesterday. She keeps asking, hoping that my answer will change or that she'll wear me down. "I'll settle down when I'm ready and meet the right man. I'm not in a rush. You know my career is important to me."

Mom isn't wrong about the holidays being lonely when you're single, but there is more to what I want from life than to get a ring on my finger and start popping out babies. I mean, yeah, of course I want a husband and I want a family, but I also want a career. Having a life *not* defined by a man and my marital status is something my mom just can't wrap her mind around, no matter how many times I've tried to explain why my career is important to me.

My mom closes her eyes for a long second, which means that she's struggling to keep her emotions in check. She thinks I'm wasting time by pursuing my career as a teacher. She also thinks my dream of becoming a school principal is as ludicrous as taking a rocket to the moon just for giggles.

"It would be better," my mother replies, then takes a dainty sip of her cocktail, "if you had a date for the ball. It doesn't look right, you going without an escort."

It's not like I *want* to go to The Sugarplum Ball without a date, but contrary to what my parents might like to believe, there is decidedly not a line of men banging down my door and asking me out for dates. It's not like anyone will know or remember if I don't have a date, since we don't actually live here and we'll never see the people there again.

My senses go on high alert when I see joy light up my mom's face and eyes. *Please. Dear God, please no.* She looks just like the cat who ate the canary...and it terrifies me. She has such a clear path she expects me to follow in my life and she completely disregards what I want. If I could have just one Christmas wish come true, it would be to have someone, anyone, encourage me to follow my heart and use my brain.

"Mom," I say, spreading those three small letters into a long drawl. I wrap my fingers tightly around the napkin on my lap and twist it so hard they tingle from lack of blood. It was beyond dumb for me to think they had a *friend* joining us. "Please tell me you haven't arranged a date for me. Please, please no."

I gulp my cocktail, cringing at the new look of triumph on my mom's face. I look imploringly at my dad, begging him with my eyes to jump in and save me, but he just smiles at me. He's a great dad, but even he won't say anything when my mom is like this.

When my parents suggested coming down to New Orleans for Christmas, and to attend a fancy holiday ball, I was happy to get out of town and leave my life behind for a little while. Though now, the wisdom of agreeing to this trip makes getting lost in a swamp sound positively delightful.

"Marian." My skin crawls at my mother's voice, low and forced through the bright smile plastered on her face. This is a fight she will never stop fighting. "It's just not right for you to go to this ball alone."

My mom willfully ignores the fact that she talks to me regularly and knows that I don't have a boyfriend.

The bigger question is *who*? It's not like we live here. We're in New Orleans for a family holiday. We don't know anyone here. If there's one thing my mom doesn't want more than me turning into a lonely old spinster, is for me to move to a different city.

I look around the fancy restaurant, wishing I could escape and not have to deal with this blind date or the ball. It was a mistake to think this would be a nice, low-stress family holiday.

"Oh! There he is now!" Both of my parents have megawatt smiles as they look past me.

I close my eyes and try to avoid noticeably cringing. At least this is just for dessert, not the full meal. That must be a silver lining. Right? Right?

"Mr. and Mrs. Copeland, it's so good to see you!"

My eyes flash open at that voice. That deep, sexy-like-melted-caramel voice. I know that voice.

"Is that Nelson Jennings?" I turn around and nearly fall on the floor when I see it *is* him. It's been more than a few years since I saw him. His parents moved to town when I was in middle school and he was a few years ahead of me. He was always running off with his friends, not hanging out with his parents' friends' awkward daughter. I was a freshman when he graduated and he immediately left for the Navy. But that voice... He had a distinctive, rich voice back then, too.

Now, I have to stop myself from drooling from the incredible power and strength emanating from him. It doesn't hurt that he's even more handsome and sexy than I remember, with his close-cut dark hair, full mouth, and piercing green eyes. His cheekbones are high and sharp enough to cut glass. He looks like a movie star, not a soldier.

"Marian. It's wonderful to see you, too."

I look at my parents and back to Nelson. I'm dumbfounded at seeing him, especially looking as handsome as he does. I haven't thought about him in years, except for the occasional update gossip my mom mentions after talking to his mom.

"What... What are you doing here? I thought you were off in the Middle East or somewhere."

"More like 'or somewhere.'" Nelson smiles as he takes the chair next to me. "My parents booked a holiday cruise down in the Caribbean, but I got some last-minute leave. My parents called your parents, and here I am."

To say that I'm dumbfounded to be sitting next to Nelson is a monumental understatement. I saw just enough of him when we were little that I knew I wanted to see more of him. Despite always loving the advantages of being an only child, I'd always wished I had a brother, so I could see Nelson more often.

"We couldn't let him spend the holidays alone, once we heard. Joan and Patrick were already off on their cruise."

Desire thrums through my body. I can't decide if this is a good thing or a bad thing. A quick glance at his left hand suggests he doesn't have a wife, but surely, he has a girlfriend somewhere. Men like him are never single.

Conversation flows easily as we have dessert, though my mother gives me several sharp looks for eating a beignet for dessert. As delicately as I can, I lick powdered sugar from my fingertips, imagining that it's Nelson that I'm licking, instead. For someone I always found intimidating and sinfully hot, it's remarkably easy to be around him. We laugh at the same jokes over dessert and I just *like* him.

"I'm so glad you could join us, Nelson. I'm sure your parents must miss you terribly." My mom gives Nelson another megawatt smile, then shoots heavy glances at me. It's obvious she's been completely charmed by him and is already planning my wedding. But I know better than to confuse politeness with romantic interest.

"It has been entirely my pleasure, Mrs. Copeland." Nelson stands and moves to my mother's chair, holding it for her as she stands up. My mother coos appreciatively, relishing being the center of attention.

"We were going to suggest going to the Audubon Zoo Lights this evening, but I'm just tuckered out. Maybe you and Marian could go?" My mother stifles a faux-yawn and I roll my eyes.

Part of me wants to kill my mom, yet part of me wants to thank her. It's not like anything serious would ever happen between Nelson and me, because we live in two extremely different worlds. I can't deny that I'm going to love spending time with him, though it already feels bittersweet because I know it's temporary.

"What do you say, Marian? Would you do me the honor of joining me?"

CHAPTER 2

NELSON

When I got the news that I was deploying home, it was a huge fucking relief. There's no other job I would rather do, because I'm fucking proud to serve my country, but there comes a time when you need to settle down and start a family. I've got plenty of buddies who have families, but moving a lot with a family can be a challenge – I've seen it with my buddies and I don't want it for myself. Besides, I want to join and support a community, not roam from country to country without ever putting down roots in one place.

What I want is a woman just like Marian to be by my side and to share my life with. I barely knew her when I was younger, and now I'm regretting it. She's smart and sweet and a knockout. One look at her tonight and I was done for – every fiber of my being understood instantly that she's the one for me.

I never would have chosen to come to this light display at the Audubon Park, but I certainly don't regret it now. There's a distinct air of Christmas, with all the lights and the carolers, and with Marian by my side, I feel like king of the goddamn universe.

"Can I ask you a question and will you be honest with me?"

"Always." I turn to face her, my groin tightening when I see her pretty cheeks flushed red in the cold night air. Marian is, hands down, the prettiest woman I've ever laid eyes on. And her body. Fuck, her body is the sexiest thing I've ever seen. Curves that go on for days and that you just want to lose yourself in over and over and over... I don't know how I could ever leave bed in the morning, if she was next to me.

"How much," she pauses and takes a deep breath. "Just how much of a setup is this? My mom is always trying to do shit..." Marian's eyes widen and she slaps her hand over her mouth. "Oh, God. I'm so sorry. I didn't mean that to sound... I mean, you're not shit. You are *so* not shit. Oh God, I'm making a fool of myself..."

By now, her cheeks are redder than a lobster and I have to shift how I'm standing because damn if her being embarrassed doesn't turn me on.

"It sounds like there was a compliment in there." I smile at her, amused at how much she's trying to hide her feelings, and impressed that she's not afraid to speak her mind. If I had any doubt about how she feels about me, it's gone.

"I..." Marian glances away, then meets my eyes. "Yes, there is a compliment in there. If I can say so, you're the nicest setup my mother has orchestrated."

I can't help but laugh at the formalness of how she's speaking.

"This probably was something of a setup, yes. This truly was last-minute leave for me and my parents *are* out on a cruise. They're not at some party I can crash."

"Yeah, Mom started dropping some heavy hints about going on a cruise, once she heard your parents were going on one," she says, her eyes still wary. "You don't have to do this, you know. I know Mom at least is hoping you'll take me to the ball, and then have you proposing to me like something out of a Hallmark movie."

"You're a spitfire, you know that?"

At this, Marian laughs and she visibly relaxes for the first time since we left the restaurant. Her blue eyes are brighter and all that's important in this moment is to keep her happy and smiling. I could die a happy man if her smile was the last thing I saw. Making her smile like this, every day and night, would be a crowning achievement in my life.

"I have to be, because of my students. They'll walk all over you if you can't keep them in line. And don't think I haven't noticed my question is still unanswered."

"I suspected this was a setup, too. God's honest truth? Moment I laid eyes on you, I was the happiest man on the planet."

"Me?" Her voice rises in pitch, surprise written all over her face. Her eyes cloud over for a split second and as much as I wish I didn't see it, I did.

"It's true." My heart pounds in my chest as I look at Marian. Her cheeks are red in the cold night air, and the way she looks under all the colored holiday lights? Fuck. I've never seen or met another woman that has one iota of the magnetism that Marian exudes – and the way she acts, I'm sure she has no idea just how stunning of a woman she's become. She was always shy as a kid, her nose always in a book, but she's come into her own. Her down-to-earth nature only makes her more appealing.

"All these displays are really pretty. Thanks for bringing me here."

I don't say anything as Marian changes the subject so baldly. She puts her hands into her pockets and pulls her coat closer.

"Are you cold?"

"I… Maybe a little," she admits, her eyes hesitantly meeting mine.

"Let me help." Before she can respond, I close the distance between us and wrap an arm around her shoulders, pulling her curves tightly against my body as we walk down a pathway lit with multi-colored lights.

At first, Marian tenses under my arm, but as we walk and dodge running children, she relaxes again. Realizing that she's comfortable is a lightning bolt to my heart.

I ask Marian about her work and it's a balm on my soul to listen to how much she loves teaching and how deeply she's devoted to the wellbeing and success of her students.

"It's on us to give children the best tools possible for their lives, so they can find their place in the world and society. We're shaping the next generation – it's how we protect this country."

By the time she finishes talking about her kids and what her goals are, her eyes are animated and she's completely at ease.

I love that she's as passionate about her work as I am about mine. Protecting our home is the most important job. Teachers are the backbone of shaping the next generation of citizens.

"Thank you for the work you do," I say, completely serious. One of the most important traits I've ever wanted in a wife is a woman who loves and supports this country as much as I do.

"What? I should be thanking *you*!"

"No, really. What you do is important and I admire you for it."

"Oh," she says, an unreadable look passing over her eyes. "Thank you. I appreciate that."

We stop in front of a brightly decorated tree and Marian's eyes have trouble and conflict written all over them.

"Marian. What's wrong? You were so excited talking about your work…and now you look like someone kicked a dog."

"It's…" Marian looks at me, then cuts her eyes away. "It's just really nice to talk to someone who's so supportive. My mom…she thinks my career is silly and that my goals are pipe dreams."

"What? That's crazy! What does she think you should be doing?"

"Honestly? She thinks I need to find a husband and give her grandchildren. She thinks a woman's greatest achievement is to be a housewife with a houseful of kids. I mean, yeah, I want to have kids and be married, eventually. I also value my career and I have big dreams for my work."

"You're so passionate about this! Of course this is what you should be doing."

"Thank you, Nelson. You really don't understand how much that means to me."

The smile she gives me is so genuine that it rights everything in the world. I'm going to make her feel safe and to help her achieve everything and anything her heart desires. Just as sure as I would lay down my life for my country and for my brothers-in-arms, I would lay my life down for her.

"Aren't you going to kiss?"

Marian and I both turn when we hear the voice of a young girl. She's standing there, one hand on her hip and the other pointing to the tree we're standing next to. We look up and see a large piece of mistletoe directly above our heads. Of course, kissing Marian is something I absolutely fucking wanting and planning to do.

Without a hesitation, I pull her into my arms, my breath catching at how perfect her curvy body feels against mine. Gently, I tilt her face up to mine, then give her the kiss I've been yearning to give her since I first saw her in the restaurant.

From the moment our lips meet, when Marian's gasp becomes an unmistakably moan and she presses her luscious body to mine, I force myself to rein in my emotions. Her lips are tender and enticingly plump, sending me to heaven the moment she parts her lips and her sweet tongue teases mine.

The sound of the little girl giggling brings us back to the real world, Marian's cheeks are high with color and making her the sexiest woman on the planet. Looking at Marian, the peace and happiness in her eyes when we're together, it reminds me why I so readily agreed to my new commission. I've travelled the world, seen the sights, had adventures. Yet now? Now I'm ready to start my family, to build a home, to build my place in a single community. I'm ready to settle down.

Marian is going to be my wife.

CHAPTER 3

MARIAN

*H*ow was everything with Nelson last night?" Mom's voice in the tourist trap gift shop is loud as she holds up two New Orleans snow globes, her expression asking for an opinion on which one to surprise Dad with.

"Aren't those a bit out of place?" I walk down a narrow aisle of cheap knick knacks, not seeing anything that really catches my eye.

"What do you mean, Marian?" My mom's voice belies a touch of impatience.

"I mean, does it even snow here?"

"Well, I…"

For a moment, I think my mom is going to snap at me, but in the end, she puts both of them down and starts to laugh, and then moves further along the aisle to the next display. I love my mom, but she can be emotionally unpredictable and demanding. It's always a relief when I can make her laugh.

"Maybe a magnet? Plus, you'll be able to get one of those through airport security."

"Perhaps so, perhaps so." Mom stops in front of a colorful display of magnets, carefully scrutinizing each of them.

I look at my mom and admire her single-mindedness. Every time she leaves town, whether they're travelling together or she's travelling on her own, she always brings back some memento for Dad. As a kid, I thought it was just clutter, but as an adult I've come to realize it's both a way to remember shared times and a way to say "I was here, but you weren't with me and I missed you, so I brought a little of where I was home for you."

As overbearing as my mom can be about me getting married and settling down, I can see why she's like that. My parents have a wonderful, strong marriage. It's what I want for myself, eventually, but not at the expense of my career. The way my mom talks, I have to choose one or the other. I've never been able to pin down if she's stuck in the 1950s, and thinks a woman's place is not in the workplace, or if she just thinks I don't have enough talent to build the career I want in education. I haven't been brave enough to ask her, because I'm scared that she thinks I'm not good enough for a career.

Thing is, I want both a career and a family, and nothing she says will ever change that.

"Well? Did you? Did you have a nice time?"

"Yes, Mom, we did. It was nice."

I smile as I think back to Nelson's kiss. When that little girl pointed out we were standing under mistletoe, I figured he'd give me a quick peck and that'd be it.

Noooo.

That kiss. It rang a bell inside me that I didn't even know was there. His kiss made me want the things my mom goes on about – and that scares me.

Nelson is a travelling man. He's in the Navy and moves all over the world. I'm a teacher and I have my spot in my community. As magical as that kiss was and as much as I really like the man he's become, falling for Nelson is something I can't allow myself to do. I need someone stable in my life, not someone who disappears for months at a time or who comes home from work and says "pack up the house, babe, we're moving to Korea for a year!"

Why, *why* can't he live closer to me?

Nelson is everything I want in a man – respectful, courteous, handsome as hell, and he has a magnetism that is irresistible. Being with him feels natural and right, and saying goodbye to him last night made me indescribably sad. I never wanted to part from him. I went to bed, fantasizing about what it'd be like to build a life with him, to become his wife.

As much as I'd have loved to 'have some fun with him,' as my best friend Katrina would suggest, Nelson isn't the kind of man you willingly let go. He's the kind of man you fight for. He's the kind of man you make lifelong plans with. If I let myself feel anything, I know I'll fall in love with him. I don't want to fall in love with a man who travels the world. I need a man who can start a family with me, be a part of our community.

I can't let myself love a man whose job sends him all over the world.

"You look so beautiful. Like a princess." I smile at my dad's compliment, my heart filling when I see the emotion in his eyes as he looks at me. I rarely have the chance to dress up like this, so it feels special that I can share a special night with him and Mom. Taking this Christmas trip with them is a special treat, as it is.

"Marian, you do look stunning." My mom looks at me appraisingly, a smile spreading across her face.

"Thank you, both of you."

I twirl in front of the mirror, pleased as I watch the deep purple of my dress flare around my legs.

"Are you two ready to go?" I wrap my new, fancy designer shawl around my shoulders, enjoying the feel of the silk around my shoulders. I was doubtful when my mother suggested it, but it's a beautiful mix of bright colors, like the Fat Tuesday masks that are for sale everywhere. It looks amazing with my dress and I feel super pretty with it on.

"We are, dear," my dad says, glancing at my mother. I look at both of them closely, instantly wary. My dad is terrible at keeping secrets and now I think I know why I've barely seen him today.

"What's going on?" My pulse starts racing and I wonder what could possibly be making my dad feel uncomfortable. After a long moment, my mom is the one to speak.

"Well, Marian," she says, coming over to me and adjusting my shawl, even though I know it doesn't need adjusting. "As I said earlier, it just isn't right that you don't have an escort for tonight."

This, again? What I would give to have my mother ease up on all the pressure for me to find a man, lose my career, and stay at home all day.

"Mom," I reply, the frustration in my voice unhidden. "What did you do?"

"I asked Nelson to be your escort."

"You what?" My voice rises sharply and it takes all my self-control to close my mouth and keep it closed.

I look at my mom and I can't decide whether I love her or hate her right now. Of course, seeing Nelson again – especially as a date for tonight – is something I'd really love. But dammit! It's only going to make me like him more, and then make it a zillion times harder to say goodbye when I fly home and he flies off to wherever he's stationed.

Why can't Mom just let me make my own decisions and lead my life, even when it doesn't match up with what she thinks my life should be? I don't even understand why she'd set me up with someone who doesn't have a place in the community.

"Don't tell me you're not a little bit excited," she says, a slight frown on her face. "I saw how you both looked at each other last night. And you were so happy and when you came back after he took you out. I just want you to be happy, sweetheart. "

"I know, Mom. I do." I sigh and give her a smile. I decide not to fight her on this. At least having a date will get her off my back for the night. "It'd just really be nice if you asked me about these things, first."

～

As I STAND at the top of the Grand Staircase of our hotel, an entrance my mother insisted I make, I nearly faint and fall down the stairs when I see Nelson.

Nelson is waiting at the bottom of the stairs, next to a massive Christmas tree loaded with lights and ornaments, looking like the best Christmas present ever. His dress blues hug his body like they were made for him, his ribbons bright against his chest, and a medal shining under the light of the chandelier. When he looks up, he stands up even straighter, a look of excitement clear on his face.

Even though I know it's not the proper way to make a staircase entrance, according to my mom, I firmly grasp the marble handrail as I carefully take each step down to where Nelson is waiting. My heart is beating so fast, I don't trust myself not to faint and fall headfirst down the stairs.

"Marian," he says, extending his arm to me when I reach the bottom of the stairs, thankfully feet first. "You look stunning."

"Thanks," I say, feeling a blush creep across my cheeks. "You look… You look magnificent in your dress blues."

"I only wear it for special occasions."

The smile Nelson gives me is dazzling and I have to remind myself this is real and not a dream. I may hate being set up by my mom, but this most definitely does not suck.

A pang runs through me when I sadly realize this is only for tonight. Regardless of Nelson being home for the holidays, he's been living abroad for the last several years and he's going to be going off somewhere new for the new year. It's going to hurt so much to say goodbye to him. After wondering if I'd ever meet a man who makes me feel special and smart and desirable, why does it have to be someone who's going to disappear to some faraway country?

I mentally shake myself, telling myself to live in the moment and enjoy his company. At least I can feel like a princess for tonight.

CHAPTER 4

NELSON

*T*he moment I saw Marian come down the grand staircase at Le Pavillon Hotel, I was even more of a goner than I was when I saw her last night. Tonight, she's an absolute vision. Her hair is done up and frames her lusciously gorgeous face, and that dress. Holy fucking hell, that dress. That purple dress hugs her tits and hips as tightly as I need to. Her body is full and womanly, and fuck if I've ever seen another woman that is one-tenth as sexy as Marian is as she came down those stairs.

"How you doing?" I ask, pulling her arm tightly against my body. She was hesitant to put her arm through mine, but when she did? Perfect goddamn fit. Mine will be the last arm she ever holds. Well, one exception. I'll watch her as she holds her father's arm as she walks down a church aisle, on our wedding day.

"I'm fine." She pauses, then looks up at me, her blue eyes piercing deep into my soul. "Well, I should amend that. I'm better having seen you, Nelson."

"I'm pleased to hear that." I'm more than pleased – I'm over the damn moon. "To be truthful, this was your mother's idea, though I said yes immediately. There is no other way I'd rather spend Christmas Eve."

The smile Marian gives me makes everything I've ever experienced worth it. All the tours on carriers or destroyers, dreaming of a life primarily on terra firma. All the uncertainty if I'd ever make it home. *When* I'd ever make it home.

And now. I'm going home and I'm going to keep this perfect woman with me. Forever.

"I REALLY SHOULD TALK to my parents, at least a little bit." Marian's voice is a giggle and her cheeks are flushed from the Hurricane cocktails we've been drinking.

"What if I don't want to let you go?" Even though the song ended and the band is taking a break, I literally cannot let go of Marian. Her body is a perfect fit against mine and I'm magnetically drawn to her. It takes more self-control than I knew I had, to hold back from taking her back to my hotel room and intimately getting to know her body.

"I wouldn't mind that." The smile she gives me is at once both innocent and seductive, and I know she's mine. I can see the war in her eyes, wanting to be with me and fighting the need to spend time with her parents.

"What if I said I wanted to see you again? Repeatedly?" I wrap my arms around her, pulling her close enough against my body that I can feel her heart pounding against mine.

Her breath catches and a look that is difficult to read passes across her eyes, and then she looks away.

"That's… That's a nice idea. Let's not shadow tonight, though. Okay?" She looks down and starts to turn her body, like she's going to walk away.

I'm not going to let her walk away, especially not after a cryptic comment like that.

"What do you mean?" Marian is unhappy about something and I'm going to fix whatever problem she has. I'll take on anyone and their army, just to make sure Marian is taken care of and safe and happy.

Marian turns back to me, her mouth set in what I assume is her 'serious schoolteacher face' that she uses with her students.

"I mean," she says, pausing to take a deep breath. Her body starts to tremble and I pull her back against my chest, holding her tightly.

"Baby, what's wrong? I thought you were having a good time, that *we* were having a good time."

"I am," she says, a sad smile on her face. "This is…last night was the best night I'd had in a long time. Tonight is even better. But I know these are just a couple of isolated nights. You're on leave," she says, her eyes meeting mine again and holding an indescribable sadness. "You're on leave, and you're going back to whatever top-secret location an officer like you, in a uniform like this, is stationed. Bremerton is my home. So, this," she says, putting her hand on my chest, her eyes still deeply focused on mine, "is just temporary."

"Marian." My voice is choked. How did she not know? How could she imagine that I would do this if I wasn't serious? "Don't you know?"

"Know what?"

"I'm not going back. I have a new commission, a permanent one. I've been stationed in Bremerton. I'm coming home. For good."

~

"Tell me about your goals."

We're sitting in the back of a horse-drawn carriage and Marian is snuggled up under my arm. Each moment that passes, it astounds me that I made it this far in life without her. How could I have lived without her? Without this kind of pure beauty and love in my life?

"Well," Marian says, wrapping her arm around me. "I really want to be a principal one day. Maybe a city administrator. I have some ideas for books, too. I love teaching – the students are like my children. It's incredibly satisfying to watch a child learn, to see how their mind unlocks when they understand an idea, and then how their mind lights up when they merge that idea with another, to come up with something new."

"I love how passionate you are about your work and students. I admire that."

"You do?"

"Of course I do. Why wouldn't I?"

"My mom doesn't," she admits, squeezing me more tightly and leaning into me. "My mom sees my job as a nice hobby to occupy my time until I settle down."

"Do you want to be married and have a family?"

"Of course I do!" Her voice is stronger and reveals a passion that resonates with me. "It's just... that's not *all* I want.

Having a career and having a family isn't an either-or proposition. My mom doesn't see it like that, though."

I lift her face up to face mine, my eyes intent on her.

"What if I do? See it like that?"

"Like my mom?" Her body tenses.

"No, like you. What if I said I'd support you in anything and everything? If you want to teach or be a city educator, that I would support you? That if you wanted to stay home with our children, that I would support you? That I would move mountains and fight an entire naval fleet single-handed, just to keep you happy. What would you say?"

"I…" Her eyes flicker between mine and my mouth. I've been dying to kiss her, to taste her, since I first laid eyes on her at the hotel, but I've forced myself to be the gentleman that she deserves. "I think this is my answer."

Marian presses her lips against mine. A possessive growl rises up in my body and I devour her kiss. Her body presses into mine and I groan as her hand moves from my chest to my hip. When her hand slides down to my thigh, I turn to her, then move her so that she's straddling my lap.

"Oh!" She pulls away from me, her breath puffing against my face. The smile on her face and the look in her eyes? It's like the universe. My universe.

"Too much?"

"Not at all."

I pull her head to mine, this time kissing her slowly. She moans as my tongue pushes against her lips, then moans louder as she opens her mouth and I stroke her tongue with mine. I reach down and cup her delicious ass with my hands, pressing her closer to my body. She grinds her hot heat down on my cock and my body quakes from the power of my need for her.

"We need to get back to the hotel."

I force an end to our kiss. The carriage is bumping down the street, the night air heavy.

"You're going to send me home?"

"No," I say, stroking her face and pushing a stray tendril of hair behind her ear. "I'm going to take you to bed."

CHAPTER 5

MARIAN

*W*e have to go back to *your* hotel," I say, pressing my body against Nelson's. His chest is so strong and muscular, and I'm drenched with my desire to touch him, to feel his skin next to mine. Every atom of my being is electrified and my need to make love with him is the deepest emotion I've ever felt. I need – *we* need – this intimacy to seal our love. "I'm sharing a suite with my parents."

"Definitely mine, then."

Nelson gives the driver the name of his hotel and I wrap my arms around him as the carriage bounces along the uneven road and under the low-hanging trees. Tonight has been magical, like something out of a fairy tale. I couldn't even have imagined a more romantic and perfect way to spend tonight.

"You know," I say, lifting my head so that I can give Nelson another kiss. "My mom is never going to let me forget this meddling of hers."

"I think I can live with that." Nelson's laugh is deep, with a pure joy to it that makes me want to listen to it forever. Everything in the world feels right with him. It's been such a tidal wave of emotions, from the annoyance at my mother meddling and setting us up – not once, but *twice*! To discovering how much Nelson and I just fit together, how we're both passionate about serving to protect and shape society.

A blush burns at my cheeks when I think of how I want to feel how our bodies fit together, too. I want to learn everything about his body – what he likes and if he's ticklish.

"Penny for your thoughts."

"I…" My cheeks burn even brighter.

"You don't have to say anymore, sweet Marian."

Nelson pulls me close and whispers in my ear.

"Are you thinking about what my skin tastes like? That's what I'm thinking about you. How your skin tastes. How your pussy tastes. What you sound like as we make love. How you sound when you come."

I smile and nod at Nelson. I can't say all these things, but it is exactly how I feel. I've never felt this way about another man. The desire to share all of me – not just my body, but also my life – is completely new to me. Love songs make sense, now.

"Good. Here's my hotel now. Let's go find out."

NELSON HAS me pinned against the wall of the old-fashioned elevator of his hotel, his breath hot against that sensitive place where my shoulder meets my neck. My body is opening up, needing to be bare against Nelson's. The power of my emotions makes me tremble in anticipation of being intimate with him.

"Finally, we're alone," Nelson says, as we walk into his hotel suite. He walks over to a French door and opens it, the sounds of music and people laughing filtering into the room with us. We're on the third floor of an historic hotel and it feels like we've joined the pulsing heartbeat of New Orleans.

"I've wanted this, too." I gasp as his fingers find the zipper for my dress and pull it down. The hairs on my arm stand up as his fingers stroke my skin and explore my body. I push my dress down to the floor, not caring if it gets wrinkled. Nelson is the most important thing right now. If I'm honest, it feels like he's going to be the most important person in my life for a very long time to come.

"I'm glad we're in agreement on this."

"You're really coming back to Bremerton?" I know the answer, but I have to ask again. Tonight is such a dream of a night that I need to keep verifying that it's real.

"I am. I would not – and will not – ever lie to you, Marian. I swear on my life."

I moan as Nelson trails a line of kisses from my jaw down to my neck. An erotic shudder overcomes me and I reach out my hand, desperate to feel his bare skin.

"Thank you." My fingers pull at the buttons of Nelson's dress uniform. The fear of damaging it makes me pull my fingers back. "I need to touch you."

I gasp as Nelson lifts his mouth and fingers from my body, immediately missing his touch.

Nelson's body, naked, is an impressive combination of height and chiseled muscles. I reach out and twirl my fingers through the dark hair on his chest, my eyes widening as my hands move over his bare skin, tracing his endless muscles.

"You are so beautiful." I gasp as I look at Nelson, pulling his head to mine so that I can kiss him. More than anything, I need to feel his body on mine, feel his body in mine. Each stroke of his tongue on mine lights a deeper fire within me.

"I need you, Nelson. So much." My voice is shaky. I give myself over to the vulnerability I feel, knowing that it will bring Nelson and I even closer.

We stumble to the bedroom, the sound of jazz music rising up from the street. The tempo of the music increases and something deep inside my body shifts, an urgency opening up inside of me. Nelson stands in front of me, naked, and he's the most glorious man I've ever seen. His body exudes power and strength, and I bite my lip when I see how big he is.

I lay back on the bed and butterflies race through my stomach as Nelson joins me. He moves his body over mine, his body heat caressing my skin.

Nelson lowers his mouth to mine and our kiss is hungry, our tongues greedy in each other's mouth. His fingers skim over my skin, tickling me and making me ache for more. I arch my back up as his fingers move lower, teasing close to my core.

I reach my hand down, my fingers finding and stroking his thick shaft, guiding him toward me. Nelson pushes into me and I cry out from his size. He plunges his thick cock deep inside of me, and it both hurts a little but also feels like the most natural and most amazing thing in the world. He's large, but I want all of it. Every stroke lights up every nerve ending in my body and it's delicious and addictive.

"That feels so good." I moan as we move our bodies together, our mouths meeting again in a hot, deep kiss. For the first time, I'm not worried about what my body looks like, because the way Nelson's eyes light up when he looks at me, it's plain as day how sexy he finds me.

"You feel amazing." Nelson gasps as he pushes even deeper inside of me. I spread my legs further, then wrap them around his waist, locking my ankles so that I can keep him inside of me. Pushing my hips up higher, a profound pleasure grows inside of me, each stroke of Nelson's cock pushing me closer and closer to the edge.

Our bodies pump and thrash together, each of us moving faster and more urgently. I find Nelson's mouth with my own, desperate to taste him with my mouth as my pleasure builds and I can feel my orgasm coming close. The moment is filled with urgency, of chasing my pleasure and making sure Nelson is as happy as he's making me.

"I want to be on top," I gasp, pushing Nelson. I've always been shy about being on top, but now? Now I want Nelson to look at me, to watch and admire how my body moves.

"Yes, ma'am!"

Nelson moans as he wraps his arms around me and flips us so that he's on his back and I'm straddling him. I take a moment to find my balance, then lace my fingers through his and rock my hips back and forth. Nelson pushes up into me and his body shakes as I increase my pace and grind down on him. All of my nerve endings sizzle with desire

Explosions start in my body and I bounce my hips over Nelson, pushing down hard so I can feel him deeply inside of me as I come.

"Oh my God! Oh my God!"

Nelson grabs me and pulls me down so that we're chest to chest, his hands moving down so they're grabbing my ass and holding me tight as he grunts and pushes up into me. My nerve endings are exploding in pure joy and feeling his pleasure sends me even further over the top. We are one.

"I love you!" Nelson calls out, wrapping his arms around me and holding me tightly as both of our bodies thrash and buck against each other, our orgasms crashing simultaneously.

"I love you, too!" I bury my face in Nelson's neck, inhaling the musky scent of him as pleasure courses through my body, making me happier than I ever imagined was even possible. Everything with Nelson feels perfect, like we are the only person the other was ever destined to be with, to love. It's scary how much I feel for him, but I know there's nothing else I can do other than show and tell him how I feel, and to build a life with him. He's the only man for me.

Our bodies relax as we regain our breath and we lay side by side on the bed, grinning at each other, the sound of jazz still filtering up to us.

"You know," I say, leaning forward to give Nelson a long kiss, "I never really thought I liked jazz. I do, though."

"I've always liked jazz," Nelson says as he runs a hand over my bare skin, his fingers exploring my body. "It'll always be our music – the music we fell in love to, the music we first made love to."

I reach down and wrap my fingers around Nelson's cock, smiling as he twitches in my fingers and he grows hard again.

"And don't forget the mistletoe." I kiss Nelson's chest as my fingers stroke and tease his cock. Nelson's eyes flutter and he pushes up into my hand. I love seeing him like this, sharing a vulnerable and intimate side of himself with me.

"Thank God for the mistletoe," Nelson agrees, shifting his body so he's over me again. "I knew from the first kiss you were the only woman for me. I love you, Marian."

"I'll love you forever, Nelson," I say, spreading my legs and welcoming him into my body again. "I love you even more than I love beignets."

"I will serve you beignets in bed, every morning for the rest of our lives, if that's what you want."

I gasp as Nelson moves slowly inside of me and a deeper set of sensations build inside of me.

"As long as we're together, all I need is you."

EPILOGUE – MARIAN & NELSON

"Next year," Nelson's whisper tickles my ear like the salty sea breeze rushing around us, "it'll just be us."

"All of us," I say, taking Nelson's hand and putting it on my stomach. I'm not showing yet and this news is our big Christmas surprise for his and my parents.

"All of us." Nelson wraps me in his arms and gives me a slow, emotional kiss. The sun is just dancing with the horizon, the sky painted in purple and gold. "Though, being on this cruise isn't bad."

"Stop," I laugh, swatting at him. "This might be great for your and my parents, but this isn't quite my style."

"Where would you rather be?"

I pause a moment. A cool breeze comes up off the ocean and I shiver, even with Nelson's arms wrapped around me.

"We should head inside, anyway. Dinner starts soon." I nudge Nelson toward the door that will lead us to the ship's grand dining room and the level of contentment I feel is overwhelming. I never imagined that I would feel so...so a part of something greater. I've felt that with my students, but it's nothing like the love relationship Nelson and I have. With my students, our relationship is temporary. Meaningful, but temporary. With Nelson, everything grows and expands, because we're permanent.

"Penny for your thoughts?"

"Just thinking of how much I love you. But to answer your question, I'd love to spend Christmas on a mountain. Maybe learn to ski. I'd love for the children to have a proper snowy Christmas. Lord knows we don't get much snow at home, at least not consistently."

"Done. Next year, the mountains."

One of the infinite things I love about Nelson is that everything is a discussion, that he's so supportive. True to his word, he stands by me as I continue to teach, encouraging me to follow my dreams, despite being pregnant. "Your career doesn't have an expiration date," is what he always reminds me. He's even stood up to my mom, which...I'd be lying if I said I didn't wish I had a video of that discussion. I think it was the first time I ever saw my mom well and truly back down from someone else. She still won't say she agrees with me having a career, but she no longer pushes me to give it up. Baby steps, I guess.

Walking through the hallways to the formal dining room, we nod at couples that we've met on this cruise. The cruise isn't so bad. It's more that I want this time to make memories of just Nelson and me. I love my family and I love his family – well, we're all one family now – but I want to cherish this time we have before our twins come next summer.

But Nelson's mom was adamant that we all spend this Christmas holiday on a cruise, together. She loved their cruise so much last year, that she insisted we all go on one this year. In the future, Nelson and I are set on hosting big family Christmas dinners at our house. We both love our big family and Christmas so much, not least because it's when we re-entered each other's life.

"You are positively beaming, Marian!" My mom gushes when we join them at our dining table. "Is that the dress…?"

I smile at my mom and run my hands over my purple dress, thrilled to be wearing it again this year. "Yes, it is the dress from last year." I look up into Nelson's dark eyes and pleasure radiates through my body."

"It's my favorite dress," Nelson adds, leaning over and giving me a kiss on the cheek.

"Well, it really becomes you."

"Thanks, Mom. You look really nice, too. Is that new?"

Mom looks down at her dress, then quickly glances at Dad. When she sees that he's deep in a conversation with Nelson's dad, she leans over and drops her voice to a whisper.

"It is! But don't tell your dad! I saw this in the boutique earlier and I just had to have it. It's my Christmas present to myself."

"Your secret's safe with me." I smile at my mom and touch her arm. While I know she doesn't agree with all my decisions, I finally feel like I'm free to make my own decisions and not have to justify them to her. She's finally treating me as an adult…well, most of the time. I've really been looking forward to see how our relationship evolves, especially when she finds out our news.

"Is that a cocktail?" She asks, arching her eyebrow as she looks at my glass, finally noticing after four out of five courses, that I'm not drinking wine. What I'm drinking is cranberry juice and orange juice, like the delicious Hurricanes I came to love in New Orleans, just minus the rum and triple sec.

I reach under the table and grasp Nelson's hand and squeeze tightly. He looks at me and smiles, and I know now's the time.

"Well," I say, drawling the word for several seconds. I can't stop grinning when Nelson squeezes my left hand back, then leans over and gives me a soft kiss on my cheek. "We have some news. We were going to wait until tomorrow night, Christmas Eve, but..."

It's moments like this when I wish I had a hidden video camera, because watching the sudden shifting of emotions on my mom's face is priceless. She starts with a wondering look, then I can see things start to click in her eyes, followed by quick glances between Nelson and me and then down to my stomach, and then a look of triumphant joy when I smile back at her and place my right hand on my stomach. Even though I'm not showing yet, it's all the confirmation she needs.

"Are you... Are you really?" The pitch of my mom's voice rises in her excitement and she rushes over to me, pulling me up so she can hug me and take a closer look at my stomach. "When are you due? Do you know if it's a girl or a boy?"

"Summer, and both." I smile at her, then pull Nelson close to me. When my mom is excited, she can be overwhelming. But with Nelson at my side, she's less overwhelming and easier to handle.

"Both?" It takes a moment, then the light clicks in her eyes and she hugs me again. "Did you hear that, honey? We're going to be double grandparents!"

The look in my dad's eyes brings tears to my eyes. He looks so proud and so happy. He's always let mom do most of the talking, but him not saying anything and letting his eyes do the talking? It hits me so deep in the feels. He and Nelson's dad both come over, slapping Nelson on the back and congratulating both of us. I fully expect them to be smoking cigars on the deck before this cruise is over.

"I'm so thrilled for you both," Nelson's mom says to me, taking me into her arms. She's a lot like my mom – overwhelming at times, but very loving and family-focused – but she's restrained from the "when are you going to make us grandparents" interrogation that my mom has done weekly since Nelson and I got married.

"Thank you." There are tears coming from my eyes now, but they're such happy tears that I don't care if they're messing up my makeup.

"You're not going to take her and the grandchildren away from us, are you?" My mom asks, after we all take our seats and the waiter brings our desserts.

"Not a chance." Nelson puts his arm around me and I lace my fingers through his. I always feel so calm and capable when we're together, like I – *we* – can handle anything, including our overwhelming moms. "When I came back last year, it was for a permanent commission. We're in Bremerton for good."

"Come here."

I look over to Nelson and he's already in bed. He's propped himself up on one elbow and the sultry look he gives me just goes straight to my heart, and then lower to my core. I thought the honeymoon phase would be over by now, but I think this intimate connection and lust we share is just...just how it is with us. It hasn't been entirely smooth sailing since that Christmas in New Orleans, but we've always been strong and grown closer after we work through things.

"How can I say no to my handsome husband?" I bite my lip when he pushes the blanket behind him, revealing his muscular naked body. The sight of him and his thick cock ratchets up the desire I've been feeling all night.

"You gotta lose the nightie, Mrs. Jennings." There's a wicked twinkle in Nelson's eyes and I don't hesitate for a second in pulling my negligee over my head.

"Is this better, Mr. Jennings?" I tease, cocking one hip to the side and shimmying. He always says I look like a pin-up model, so I always do my best to pose like one. It's one of our little things and something I cherish, not to mention it's given me a ton of self-confidence in my body.

"It will be better when you're next to me." Nelson's voice is heavy with desire and my body is already responding to him.

"Well, if you absolutely insist."

I crawl into bed and there is nothing but happiness in my world. I love Nelson, he loves me, and the beginning of our family is in my belly.

"You are a perfect man. You know that, right?" I give my husband a slow, deep kiss, my hands stroking his muscular body. I run my fingernails lightly over his waist, smiling when I feel him twist and shudder. If you'd have asked me if I thought a big, muscular Navy officer was super ticklish, I'd never have guessed. But Nelson is and I love tickling him.

"I'm a perfect man because you're a perfect woman. I wouldn't be the man I am if it wasn't for you." Nelson moves so that his body is above mine and I instinctively open myself up to him. Any fear of showing him all of me, both physically and emotionally, is long gone. He's seen me and he loves me exactly as I am. He's so much more than I ever expected to find for myself.

"I love you." I pull Nelson down to my waiting body, shuddering with pleasure as he enters me. Our love is the foundation of our life and I couldn't be happier.

UNWRAPPING HER CURVES

CHAPTER 1

MANDY

At this rate, I'll be lucky to get home by New Year's Eve.

"Hey, Jimmy."

"Hey, Sis. Where you at? Should I crack open a beer for you?"

I crane my neck out into the cool afternoon air, then groan.

"I wish. No. I'm still on the freeway. It's…"

"What have I told you about phones while driving? You know how many people I take to the ER because of distracted driving!"

"Whoa. We're at a literal standstill. In fact, my motor is off – just like everyone else. There must be an accident somewhere up the road, because I can't see where the backup even begins. I'm just calling to say I'm going to be phenomenally late."

"Jeez. Sorry. It's just—"

"It's okay. I know. I haven't forgotten the stories you've told me."

"You should save your phone battery. Text me when it starts clearing and when you have an idea of when you'll arrive. And call me if you need anything." The tone of Jimmy's voice is more somber. It's not the time of year to get stranded on the side of the road. It's not snowy, yet, but it's not at all warm.

"Yes, Dad," I say, a smile spreading across my face. "I'll keep you posted. And don't go bogarting all the beer, 'k?"

SITTING in traffic leaves me alone to think, which is something I've been avoiding lately. The holidays are always hard, primarily because Jimmy and I lost our parents four years ago, thanks to a drunk driver on Christmas Eve. I'm also not as excited as I feel I should be, because my 'I think this guy is the one' boyfriend dumped me three weeks ago.

I know everyone will look at me, that tinge of pity in their eyes when I say that I'm single, *again*. The common refrain will be something like "You're a catch!" or "You'll find someone when you least expect it!" or "You're smart and pretty...it will work out next time!"

It seems like there's always *next time* on the horizon, when what I really want is to settle down and start a family. No one seems to understand why all of my relationships don't work out — least of all *me*. What's sad, is that I've figured out what the common denominator in all these relationships is – it's me. I don't know how to figure out what's wrong with me, so I can fix it and move on.

Frustration runs through my body and I sit, tense, as I watch the endless lines of red brake lights in front of me. *This traffic jam is not unlike my love life – stalled and going nowhere fast.* I say a little prayer for whatever is causing the traffic jam, because it's likely an accident and someone is seriously hurt.

I BREATHE an enormous sigh of relief when I pull into my brother's driveway. I need a beer or three after that drive. My gas tank is nearly empty, my butt is sore, and my jacket isn't enough against the chilly wind that blasts me as I hoist my suitcase out of my trunk and rush up to my brother's house. I smile as I knock on the brightly lit front door.

I'm looking forward to moving home in February, and then starting a fresh life. I've been stuck in a pattern of men who aren't right for me and I haven't figured out how to find one who *is* good for me. It's just, sometimes, it's easier to get blinded by lust or dating someone you *think* should be right for you.

I knock on the door hard, again, eager to get inside and see my brother.

When the door opens, my body stops shivering as my libido flares bright enough to heat the whole of Oregon. I blink my eyes rapidly, wondering if car fumes got to me and I'm hallucinating.

"What the hell are *you* doing here?"

CHAPTER 2

TREVOR

*W*ell, hello to you, too, Mandy Hunter. Are you enjoying the holiday season?" I grin, delighting in Mandy's reaction when at seeing me. I gave specific instructions for Jimmy not to tell anyone I'd be home this year, but I wasn't sure if he'd actually keep his word on that.

Mandy marches past me, cheeks red from the cold and her eyes bright, and a bolt of desire goes straight to my groin.

Holy fuck.

I knew she was coming, but I didn't realize how amazing she looks now. Our paths haven't crossed in years, since I've always been in a stadium, playing a game on Christmas Day.

If I'd realized Mandy was all sexy and soft curves, I'd have made it back home years ago. She's the one I always wanted, the one who always said no and forever teased me. Fuck. I've spent years fantasizing about her.

"Hey man, close the door! That wind is freezing!"

"Yeah, sorry, Jimmy." I close the door behind me, I turn and see Mandy staring at me.

"Hey, Mandy. How are you? It's been a long time." I move closer to her, to give her a hug, but the expression on her face rapidly cycles between surprise, what I hope is lust, and then a wall comes down in her eyes. Obviously, she has a boyfriend waiting for her or coming along in a day or two. I've heard about her, occasionally, from Jimmy, and there's no way someone as smart and gorgeous as she is could be single.

"Yeah, I'm fine. I..." she mumbles, her blue eyes quickly cutting away from mine. It stings when she looks toward the living room and walks away from me. No one ever walks away from me.

"Sis! You made it!"

"Barely," she sighs, shrugging off her coat and throwing it on a side chair. "Hey Grace. I'm so glad to see you! It's been too long since I saw my best friend!" She gives everyone else a big hug and jealousy rises up in me something fierce.

"It's about time you got home, sis." Jimmy hugs her with one arm and passes her a bottle of beer with the other. "Didn't run out of gas?"

"No," she says. Damn... Watching her tilt that bottle back and take a long drink? A rush of blood goes straight to my groin as I envision her lips wrapped around my cock. Mandy was always sexy, in her shy way, but Jimmy made it damn clear she was off limits.

Now? We're all grown up and it's time for the rules to change.

"WHAT *ARE* you doing back here, Trevor? I thought you were living your best life as a famous football player."

I look at Mandy, relieved that she's finally talking to me. We weren't on bad terms last we saw each other, but there's been something dark in her eyes every time I've seen her looking at me tonight. It's like she has a grudge against me, though I know that's impossible. I haven't seen her in years.

"I suppose I was." No matter how many times I'm recognized in public or get interviewed on television, I just feel like me, that talented kid from Gresham. I don't feel like a superstar, though playing pro football has definitely had some Hollywood moments. "I hurt my knee again last month and I'm on the DL. Since I can't play on Christmas, I came home."

"Huh." Mandy's eyes are unreadable as she looks at me, but at least she no longer looks like she wants to kill me. Still, there's a definite distance between us.

"What about you? How you doin' in the big city?"

"Don't ask." She rolls her eyes and takes another long pull of her beer. "In fact, I dislike it so much, I'm moving back here in February. I wanted to come back earlier, but work locked me into a final project. Honestly, I can't wait to come home, even if it means seeing my obnoxious brother all the time."

Mandy smiles at her brother, leaning over to punch him on the arm. Jimmy laughs, punching her back on the arm.

"Yay!" Grace's voice is a screech of excitement and she lunges over to Mandy and gives her a big hug. "You didn't tell me you had a finalized move date! I can't wait for you to be back!

You won't regret it, girl, seriously. Oh my God! I can't believe I'm finally getting my BFF back!"

Once again, a shadow falls over her eyes. There's a story she's not telling people. I want to ask her, but I know better than to ask her in front of the others. Though, I tell myself, why would she even talk to me? She has absolutely zero reason to confide in me and with the way she's been looking at me, I seriously doubt she has any plans to.

Maybe she's heard about the reputation I had a few years ago. A lot of money and a lot of fame doesn't lend itself to respectable behavior. I fell into the fame trap that so many of us did – lots of parties, booze, women, money to burn, acting like kings because everyone treated us as kings. Looking back, I'm grateful I didn't get in any trouble and I didn't end up with a surprise baby from a woman I didn't remember.

These days, I want a nice quiet life, to give back to the community that helped me become the football player I became. I want to be married and have a big family.

As I watch Mandy relax in front of the fireplace, laughing and joking with her brother and Grace, I'm reminded even more why I liked her. She's funny and down to earth, not to mention the shape of her body. I feel damn lucky to be a part of this. She's natural, here, the love for her brother and best friend plain as day remind me why I always found her so compelling.

Mandy is exactly the kind of woman I want for a wife. I finish another beer, then am blindsided by the realization – it's Mandy. It's always been Mandy. Even when she turned me down, time after time in high school, it was always her. Some part of me, deep down, knew that she was the one. She was the only girl I ever longed for enough that I kept asking and asking.

She's the woman I want to be my wife.

CHAPTER 3

MANDY

*O*h, no...I don't think about Trevor..." Grace says, nearly falling on the floor because she's laughing so hard. "Mandy, babe, you should hear yourself. I don't need a polygraph to know you're lying when you say that!"

"Well...maybe," I finally concede. "Okay, maybe a lot. But you know how it is! He's on TV, he's in the paper, he's in magazines. Like chunky me would ever have a chance with him. As if!"

I drain the rest of my beer and motion to the bartender to bring us two new beers.

"Again, with the lies! Don't think I've forgotten how he chased after you in high school or how you teased him. He wanted you *bad* and I know how hard you crushed on him."

"You of all people know how much I wanted him back then. But he was so busy having everyone else and was so famous for never dating a girl for more than one or two weeks."

I look away from Grace and lose myself in the memories from high school. Me, being the 'girl with a pretty face,' but not 'the girl that every guy wants to date.' It's not that I was even that much overweight, but that I wasn't as skinny as the popular girls. And for that, I was never fully part of the in crowd. I wasn't with the outcasts or the loners, but I was in that weird middle ground of 'not quite good enough.'

Aside from my work, most of my life has felt like 'not quite good enough.' I've certainly felt that way with men, who inevitably dump me and said cliché things like "you're really pretty" or "I'm just not ready for a relationship" or "you haven't done anything wrong." And then I run into them six months or maybe a year later and what's the status then? They're engaged. They're recently married. It always leaves me feeling like shit.

"Girl, I think you did the right thing in high school. He was too popular for his own good. Despite how much he obviously wanted you, he would've broken your heart like he did with all the other girls."

"Maybe you're right. But I'm still the same. Since he went pro, all he's had are a string of flings or high-profile girlfriends. And we both know that I can't fill those kinds of shoes. Or rather, I can't fit in those kinds of dresses."

"I don't know, Mandy. You shouldn't be so down on yourself." The look in Grace's eyes changes to the look of concern that she gives me every time the subject of me and men come up. Her telling me how beautiful I am and how amazing I am, in an attempt to boost my self-esteem, is a well-worn talk that I don't believe anymore. It's not like I don't know these things, but it's hard to believe them when I have yet to meet a man who feels the same way.

"I know what you're going to say, Grace, and I love you for it, I really do. But I've just been dumped yet again. So, yeah. My self-esteem has taken yet another beating."

Sadness and anger flip across Grace's eyes as she watches me. "Are you okay? You didn't even tell me that you were dating anyone."

I sigh and silently curse how beer loosened me up enough to admit this. My mind immediately plays the highlights reel of my short relationship with Robert. We had our good moments and he knew how to make me laugh, but he didn't like taking me out with his friends or with his coworkers.

"Things weren't always great between us. I liked Robert, but I think I probably knew that it would never work out with him, but I still hoped. When I asked about his corporate Christmas party, he got all weird and said they couldn't bring dates. I think he just meant he was embarrassed to be seen with me."

"What a bastard!" Grace is suitably outraged on my behalf and as much as I didn't want to tell the story, her having my back and denouncing Robert does make me feel a little better.

"Pretty much."

"Have I mentioned he's a fucking asshole? Oh!" Grace exclaims, her eyes glittering with calculation, "that just means that now is the best time to have a fling. And who better to have a fling with than Trevor Collins? I'd bet my right arm that he would make you feel ah-mazing. I saw how he was looking at you last night. He couldn't take his eyes off you."

"There's way too much history there. He's my brother's best friend and I'll definitely see him in the future. I don't need to add to my future stress. Plus, you know I'm not the type to have flings with men." A hazy lust-dream settles in my mind – Trevor, naked and smiling in my bed, his hand outstretched to me in invitation, me taking his hand, and then me losing myself in him and making every sexual fantasy I've ever had a reality.

"And that there is a damn shame, Mandy Hunter."

"No fair that you get the pro football player on your team!" I yell at my brother, pretending I'm upset.

We're choosing sides for our annual flag football game. The sun is as high in the sky as it gets in December, but it's the prettiest, clearest day I've seen in weeks. Bright blue skies, a not-too-cold breeze, no hint of rain or snow in the air. It's perfect.

"You gave me first pick. What did you think was going to happen?" He puts his hands on his hips and smiles gleefully at me. "Besides, I'm not an idiot. I know how fast you run!"

"Are you saying you want me?" Trevor teases, walking over to me. I jump when he slides his hand down my back and dangerously close to my ass.

"What gave you *that* idea?" I faux-pout at him as I dance away from his hand and the warmth of his tight body. Trevor's caress triggers a fresh wave of desire in me and I really want to tackle him...naked.

At halftime, Jimmy passes around a couple of thermoses filled with rum-laced hot chocolate. The alcohol warms my body and helps me to relax a little. Every time I get close to Trevor, I fumble and stumble because I'm so distracted by his tall, muscular body. No matter how much I tell myself to stop with all the fantasies, I can't deny that I'm more attracted to him than I was in high school – and that's saying something!

"Alright! For the win!" Jimmy dances around on the field, celebrating that he and Trevor are up by ten points.

"Yeah, yeah. Just you wait," I taunt, putting my hands on my hips. "Grace and I are going to destroy you."

Jimmy looks at Trevor, and then busts out laughing. "Yeah right, little sis. You're playing against two pro football players!"

"Two? I think you're mistaken there, dear brother. Because from where I'm standing, I only see one pro."

"Fine. If it wasn't for this damn shoulder, I would've been a pro player too. You know that."

"Coulda woulda shoulda." I laugh in the cool breeze, walking over to where Trevor and Jimmy are standing, ready to start the second half of the game.

Jimmy lowers his eyes at me and I know he's going to come at me hard. We start the second half and Grace and I nearly tie up the score.

"Just admit it, Mandy," Trevor says joining in with Jimmy and heckling Grace and me. "You know we're going to win."

We'll see about that. The play starts and Jimmy sprints with the ball. I chase after him as fast as I can, but Trevor steps in front of me suddenly and blocks me. I slam into his body and we both go flying onto the ground, and I land on top of his strong body.

"Oof!" The air goes out of my lungs and it takes me a hot second to realize that I am lying on top of Trevor Collins. A million thoughts run through my mind, namely that I must be crushing him. "I…um… Sorry about that. I didn't mean to tackle you. But you just got in my way."

I squirm to try and move away from him and stand up, but he grips my arms so that I can't move.

"I was just doing my job and blocking you." Then in a quieter voice, he adds, "but if this is what it takes to get close to you, then I'll step in front of you every time I see you. You can tackle me any time. Any time at all."

"I think you should let me get up, so that we can continue the game," I say, flustered. Of all the ways I imagined being body to body with Trevor, this isn't what I imagined.

"But what if I don't want to let you go? I've always wanted you. You know that."

The tone of Trevor's voice gives me pause. There's a seriousness to his voice that I've rarely heard, and even though the warning bells in my mind are telling me to run away, I just want to sink into something with Trevor — preferably a bed.

"I don't know…" There aren't many times in my life where I've been at a loss for words, but I can't think of anything coherent to say. I can hear Grace and Jimmy laughing and talking, but I can't register the actual words. Right now, my whole world is what Trevor is saying to me and the way his body feels under mine.

Trevor and I stand up, but we can't stop looking at each other.

"Are you okay?" Trevor's voice is gentle and it sends a whole new set of emotions in motion for me. He's always been brash and arrogant, but there's a tenderness right now that hits deep inside of me.

I look away as I brush off my clothing. "I think so, yes. How about you? Did I crush you?"

"I've never been better," he says, looking deep into my eyes. "Let's go for a beer after the game. Just you and me."

A million thoughts race through my mind. I know what he's asking and I know that I should say no, but my body and my self-esteem need this. Maybe I need to abandon my fear of flings and just have a fling with him. I ignore the voice that says "what about when you see him in the future" and smile at him.

"Yes."

CHAPTER 4

TREVOR

*T*his game can't end fast enough.

I want to lose myself in Mandy and her luscious body. I want to hear her sigh and moan as we roll around in bed and take care of what I wish we'd taken care of so many years ago. She said no to me so many times back in the day, that it *really* feels like Christmas has come early. Her saying yes to a drink feels better than winning the Super Bowl.

"What's gotten into you man?" Jimmy asks. "You're barely passing me the ball."

I wipe my arm across my forehead. "I'm scoring, right?"

"Sure. But were supposed to be a team, right?" Jimmy's voice is tight.

"Sorry, man. Next one's yours."

I get the ball and run to the side, easily evading Mandy and Grace. Jimmy runs long and is wide open. I throw the ball to him and it sails perfectly through the air. He's going to make a touchdown easily, because Mandy and Grace are trying to block me and completely ignoring him.

"What?" Grace says, her eyes tracking the ball. "Dammit."

I watch as Jimmy reaches to catch the ball. Mandy is sprinting toward him and she might just catch him.

"Get it, man!" I yell.

Jimmy jumps for the ball, but his timing is off. He stretches for the ball and fumbles it, and I wince as he falls and lands on his arm. Hard.

I immediately run over to Jimmy because I know what a bad fall looks like. He's slow to get up off of the ground and his eyes are screwed up in pain. This isn't good. I recognize how hard he's trying hard to mask his pain, but the way he's swearing shows how badly he's losing the battle.

"Dude. You okay?"

"Jimmy! Are you okay?" Mandy asks, breathless.

Jimmy groans and starts to sit up. "I dislocated my fucking shoulder again." He stands up and wrenches his shoulder back into place, bellowing as he does so. Resetting your own shoulder is excruciating.

"Dude, we need to get you to the hospital."

Jimmy tries to resist, but when he tries to make a fist and only manages to faintly grasp at the air, it's glaringly obvious that he needs the ER.

"That's it. Don't try and argue with me. We're going to the hospital." The look in Mandy's eyes is pained when she sees how much her brother is hurting. She's already walking to the car, assuming that we're following her.

"Fuck, man. I think I pinched a nerve." Jimmy's eyes are rolling back in his head and I wince, worried he's about to pass out. We follow her and she sets off for the hospital like a bat out of hell.

"Almost there, buddy." Mandy speeds through the traffic. Every bump in the road on the way to the hospital makes Jimmy groan like a dying man. "I know this isn't the greatest time to say this, but this is why you shouldn't try to deal with your shoulder on your own."

"I know, I know. Damn shoulder is why I never got a shot at playing pro."

"You'll be fine in a few weeks. This next week, you need to keep that arm in a sling. No exceptions." The doctor narrows her eyes at Jimmy. "You remember what happened last time you didn't follow my orders, right?"

Jimmy looks sheepish as he looks up at the pretty doctor. This is obviously not the first time she's set Jimmy's shoulder for him. If she is who I think she is, she's the one that nearly put him in a hard cast after he played a game when his shoulder wasn't healed and he came back less than a week after she had set it.

"Yes, ma'am. Don't worry. I know I'm not getting any younger. Besides," he grins, his eyes starting to sparkle from the effects of the painkiller they gave him, "I can get these two here to do the Christmas cooking. That'll be fun to watch."

"What?" Mandy's voice rises to a shrill pitch that makes everyone wince. "I can handle all the cooking just fine."

"Tell that to the ham you scorched three years ago."

Mandy grumbles and looks away from Jimmy, embarrassment coloring her cheeks.

"I like to cook, though I'm not always the most attentive... and sometimes things get burnt." Mandy doesn't look me in the eye as she says this and it takes all my self-control to not smile. In high school, she always had this persona of having everything together and being in control, even though I knew from Jimmy that that wasn't really the case.

"Trevor, man. Make sure she doesn't kill the ham. It's not Christmas without ham. Don't kill the ham. Please?" Jimmy's eyes are drooping and whatever they gave him for the pain is kicking in strong.

"Can *you* even cook?" Mandy challenges me, her eyes narrowed and highly skeptical.

I step closer to Mandy, my eyes locked on hers. "I know how to do more with my hands than just throw a football."

The blush that flames across her face makes me smile and makes my cock vibrate with desire. I'm gonna have permanent blue balls if I can't get her alone and naked sometime soon. I need to be close to her, because I need to know if she feels the way I do.

Mandy eventually cuts her eyes away and it thrills me to see just how flustered she is.

"Okay. Fine. Let's take Jimmy home, then you can buy me that beer and tell me about these supposed mad cooking skills you have."

"Deal."

"AND THAT," I push a paper coaster with a dinner menu listed on it toward Mandy, "is how I think we should do Christmas dinner."

Mandy looks at me, then looks back down at the menu. She lets out a low whistle and shakes her head. Her auburn hair falls in her face and I instinctively reach out and gently push it behind her ear.

"Oh!" Mandy jumps like she's been electrocuted. Even though she's not saying a word, she's studying me closely, a million emotions and thoughts racing across her pretty face.

Seeing Mandy squirm makes me want her even more. Little by little, her tough girl façade is cracking. I know she wants me, but I know I also have to work for it. One bad play and she'll be saying no to me for the million and tenth time.

"Are you okay?" I turn my bar stool so I'm facing her and put my hand on her knee. Her eyes follow my hand and my heart isn't the only thing pounding when she puts her hand on mine.

"Oh, I think I'm quite okay. Don't you?" She smiles at me, her cheeks red from the beer and the heat of the bar.

"I think you're more than okay," I say, leaning closer toward her. Something has shifted in her, whether the beer or something else, but no way in hell am I going to ask her what changed – I'm just thankful that she's opening herself up to me. I curve my hand so that it's on the back of her knee, then I pull her knee out so that I can stand up in front of her, between her legs. "In fact, I think you're quite spectacular."

"You don't say, Trevor?"

I see the smile on her lips and know that I'm a goner. Her lips are full and perfect.

"I've been saying this for years. Or don't you remember?"

"Maybe I need a little reminding. Perhaps you—"

"OH MY GOD! Trevor Collins! Is that really you?"

I take a deep breath and turn my head toward a shrill voice I recognize in an instant. Jessica Yarrow.

Fuck.

"Jessie. How ya been?"

I watch Jessie look at me, then at Mandy, then to my hand on Mandy's knee. Jessie's forehead creases and she tilts her head.

"I'm well. Why don't you come over, talk with me a few minutes?" Jessie bats her eyes. That used to mean something to me, in high school, but it doesn't phase me anymore. "You don't mind, do you Mindy?"

"It's Mandy." Mandy's voice is tight.

"No thank you," I say, aggravated at how Jessie flicks her blonde hair and turns so that she's facing me, and aggressively ignoring Mandy.

"Come on over, please? You can join us, too, Mandy."

"No. We were just leaving, weren't we Mandy?"

Mandy looks at me, confusion and upset on her face. My parents raised me to be polite, but I will be rude to Jessie if I need to. I'm here with Mandy and she's the only person important to me right now.

"Sorry about that," I say once we're in the parking lot and away from the bar. "Let's go somewhere else."

"No, that's okay. I'm going to head home." The sadness in her voice kills me. I'd do anything to make this right, but reading her body language doesn't take a pro football player to read. She's glancing toward her car and the sexy vibe we had going is gone. Fuck.

CHAPTER 5

MANDY

*H*ow's your brother doing?" Grace asks as she parks her car in the crowded mall parking lot. We're on a mission for toys for her nephew.

I roll my eyes at Grace.

"That bad, huh?"

"I'll let you guess," I sigh. "He's not doing anything big...yet, but that's just a matter of time. I love my brother, but he has no idea when to slow down. I'm scared that one day he won't be able to bounce back fully."

"Men." Grace shakes her head, a rueful smile on her face.

"Brothers!"

"Oh, speaking of men," Grace grins, threading her arm through mine as we navigate through cars and families in the parking lot. "Do tell about you and Trevor. That tackle of yours was...let's just say you were heating up the whole city there for a minute!"

I can't help from smiling at the memory of Trevor. The feeling of his ripped body beneath mine was fantastic.

"My God he's hot."

"Hot, and totally and only has eyes for you, babe. What happened with you two after you took your brother to the hospital?"

The memory of last night at the bar wipes the smile off my face. Grace looks at me when I don't immediately respond and her smile falters.

"Uh oh. What happened? Because by the look on your face, what everyone *thought* was going to happen clearly didn't."

"Yeah, no. I slept alone last night." I tug my scarf so that it fits more snugly around my neck, then pull Grace faster toward the mall. "Let's get inside. It's cold out here."

"Uh oh. What happened?"

I tell Grace about the flirting and how it ignited something in me, something more than just lust, and how I really, really wanted to sleep with him, but how Jessie showed up and killed the mood.

"Wait. You were going to go home with him? You always pushed him away, in high school. Not to mention you're just out of a relationship..."

"Yes, you're right on both points. But it just felt different, you know?" I point at a truck set, but Grace shakes her head and we keep moving down the toy aisle. "There was something more between us, more than just sexual fizz. We may live in different cities, but...I don't know. Maybe I was hoping for something more."

Grace turns and laughs at me, her face breaking into a smile as she starts laughing.

"What?"

"*Maybe.* Girl, you should hear yourself. There was no maybe in your voice. Something has been brewing between the two of you for *years*. I thought maybe it would finally happen with you two – and I'm not just talking about banging hot sex!"

A grandmother looks at us and I mouth *sorry*. To Grace, I say, "Keep your voice down. We don't need everyone knowing about my failed shot with Trevor."

"Sorry," Grace says. "What do you think of this?" She points at a mini foosball set.

"That looks like fun. Is he old enough for that?"

"Yeah." Grace grabs the big box and we head for the front of the store and the cashiers. "But what about you? Are you going to be okay? Are you going to see him again?"

This time, it's my turn to start laughing. "Oh, Grace. I didn't tell you about what happened at the hospital."

"Oh, no. I thought everything was okay?"

"What? Oh, Jimmy will be fine, as long as he follows the doctor's orders. I mean more like Jimmy can't cook Christmas dinner like he's been planning."

"God, I hadn't even thought of that. What are you going to do? Are you just going to go out? Get some catering in?"

"Well, if only it was that easy!" I laugh again, enjoying how it feels. "No. Jimmy immediately said that dinner is on Trevor and me."

"What?!"

"Exactly. Last night, he even came up with an amazing menu plan. I think he really does know how to cook."

"That's good, because…" Grace looks at me, the apology in her eyes.

"Yeah, yeah. I know. I'm not Sally Homemaker when it comes to cooking, alright?"

Grace shakes her head and lets out a low whistle. "Are you going to be okay with that? You're not going to be able to escape seeing him. If it was me, that would be awkward as hell…"

"Tell me about it. But I don't see another option. I'm certainly not going to abandon my brother on Christmas and certainly not when his arm is messed up and he has to take it easy."

The idea of Trevor Collins, star quarterback for the Austin Blues, in a kitchen with an apron on? Oh yeah, that's hot. H-O-T. I've always dreamt of having a boyfriend who cooked for me, which sadly has so far been nothing but a dream.

"I'll do what I can to help, you know. Not sure I can do anything, but even if it's just faking an emergency that needs your help, I've got your back." Grace gives me a hug as we wait in the check-out line.

"You're the best," I whisper to her, emotions rising in me. A lot of the time, it feels like I'm lost, like I should have figured out life already.

"No, you are…even if you can't cook to save your life."

I smile and hug her tighter.

"My cooking isn't that bad!"

~

"HEY, SIS. HOW YA DOIN'?"

Jimmy's laid out on the couch, one arm in a sling and another holding on to a bottle of beer.

"Doing alright." I kick off my shoes and go to the end of the couch, making him move his feet. "How's your shoulder feeling? Are you really supposed to be drinking beer with those painkillers?"

I love my brother, and as an EMT he should know better, but sometimes he's foolish.

When Jimmy mutes the game he's watching, I know something serious is up. I offer up a quick prayer that he hasn't had bad news from the doctor.

"So. Mandy. What's going on with you and Trevor?"

I freeze. I've never really been comfortable talking about guys with my brother, and I'm not sure I want to start now – especially about Trevor.

"Uh…nothing. Nothing is happening."

"Sis, don't try to lie to me. There's been something between you two since high school. You looked ready to hump him on the field yesterday. But today, you've been smiling, but I can tell you're not happy. What's wrong? Do I need to go teach Trevor a thing or two about messing with my sister?"

"You couldn't throw a half-decent punch if your life depended on it," I laugh, pointedly looking at his injured arm.

Jimmy looks at his sling and laughs with me.

"In any case, nothing is going on. Honestly." I'm not going to tell my brother about how Trevor was touching my leg last night or how I was ready, as he so eloquently put it, hump the living daylights out of him.

"I'm not sure I believe you," Jimmy finally says, giving me a long look. "You gonna be okay with him around and helping him with Christmas dinner? Just because I can't cook doesn't mean Christmas dinner is off."

This has been the thing I've thought about most of the day. Can I face Trevor after last night? Do I even want to? I wasn't lying when I told Grace that I can't and won't abandon my brother. That's not what family does, and my brother is more important than whatever is, or *isn't*, going on between me and Trevor.

I take a deep breath and nod my head. "Yeah, I'll be fine."

"Good. Because he's on his way over, so you can go do the shopping for the dinner."

CHAPTER 6

TREVOR

*H*i, Trevor." Mandy's voice is tight when she greets me at the door and it's obvious something is wrong.

Inside, it's obvious that there's something going on with her brother, though he's grinning.

"So, you're here to take me grocery shopping?" Mandy says, pulling on her coat. "Let's get it over with."

I look at Jimmy, but he keeps on smiling and shrugs, in a *don't argue, man, just do it* way. Taking on three-hundred-pound guys on the field is easy compared to being around a woman who's upset.

"Yeah, I thought we could try and get a jump on the crowds. Seems Jimmy, here," I smile, trying to inject some levity in the room, "did not stock up before blowing out his shoulder."

Mandy glares at Jimmy, who's stretched out on the couch, beer in one hand and remote control resting on his stomach.

"Don't blame me. I don't mind all the crowds."

Something that sounds a lot like *whatever* comes from Mandy, then she's quickly walking to the door.

I pause when we get outside. "You want to drive?"

Right now, the main goal is to find out what's going on and to try fix whatever is wrong.

"Yeah, I'll drive. Get in."

Mandy doesn't speak until we get to the grocery store.

"Look. I'll admit I need help cooking Christmas dinner. But let's just stay out of each other's way, okay?"

"Mandy, what's wrong?" The vibes she's sending off are explosive. Whatever is under her skin is deeply under her skin.

"What?" Mandy looks at me and pauses, the look on her face softening just a little. "No, it's fine. I just wasn't expecting… any of this. It's been a hard month. I'll be fine."

"You sure?" She doesn't look fine and knowing her, I don't believe that she will be anytime soon.

"Yeah. Let's get going."

"ALRIGHT. That's everything from my list," I say, doublechecking the mountain of food in the cart. "Is there anything else you need? Might as well stock up since we're here."

"Um, yeah. Hold on. Why don't you get in line?"

"Sure thing."

I maneuver toward the snaking lines by the cashiers and let myself feel a little bit of hope. Mandy's discomfort thawed a little as we shopped and I *think* this won't be the most awkward thing I've ever done.

It takes longer than a minute for Mandy to return and when she does, her arms are loaded down with boxes and bags of fruit.

"Why didn't you grab a basket?" I ask, shaking my head as I help her put everything in the cart.

"I didn't think I would see so much I wanted or that Jimmy probably needs." There's a sweet *oof* to her voice as she drops the last of her last-minute shopping in the cart. It warms my heart that even though she was upset with her brother when I picked her up, she's still thinking of him and showing how she cares by making sure he has what he needs.

I'm grateful when we make it through the cashier's line and out to the parking lot without people coming up to talk to me. I don't mind talking to fans, but all I want right now is to be with Mandy, without being interrupted. I need her to know that she comes first.

I put all the groceries in the trunk while Mandy warms up the car.

"Okay. That's done." I close the door behind me, grateful for the warmth of the car.

Mandy's doesn't notice as I pull something special out of my pocket.

"Hey. Hold up a sec. There's something else."

Mandy's sigh is irritated and she turns the car off. "What now?"

I pull the mistletoe I bought out of my pocket and place it above our heads.

"This."

I pull Mandy into a kiss and an erotic charge goes straight to my groin. For a moment, her body is tense, but then her body melts against mine. Her lips are soft and sweet, and I have to restrain myself from just devouring her. Yet when she opens her mouth and her delicious little tongue darts out and touches mine, I let myself go. Weaving my fingers through her silky auburn hair, I hold her tightly and plunge my tongue deeper into her mouth. Mandy moans and kisses me back fiercely.

It feels like being a teenager again, making out in a car. This is exactly how I wish it had been between us in high school, if only I hadn't been such an idiot and scared of her brother. I haven't felt awkward about a woman in a very long time. Though when the woman is your best friend's little sister, you can't help but be nervous.

I lower one of my hands to inside of her coat and she pushes her breast into my hand. Even her thick sweater can't hide how exquisitely hard her nipple is under my fingers.

"We should—"

A sharp honking interrupts us and we look up to see a driver glaring at us, aggressively motioning in a "get out or get moving because I want your parking spot" way.

"We should get home, yes." Mandy's voice and hands tremble.

As I put my hand on hers as she starts the car, the smile she gives me lets me know it was worth it to her, too.

This is going to be the best Christmas ever.

CHAPTER 7

MANDY

*W*hat was that?" My voice warbles as I try to catch my breath, my heart thumping like it's going to burst out of my chest.

Trevor's smile is slow and gorgeous across his mouth. "That, Mandy, was a kiss in the tradition of Christmas and mistletoe."

"That was not just a friendly Christmas kiss," I protest. I don't know what's going on. I liked the kiss. No, I *loved* the kiss. But how is he attracted to me? We're not in high school anymore and I'm definitely not the kind of woman he dates – I've seen all the pictures online of his girlfriends. There's this weird push-pull going on between us and it's confusing as hell.

But kissing him… It filled my heart and soul with happiness. It was a kiss with more than passion – it held *promise*. I was expecting *fun*, not something that…not a kiss that felt more meaningful than any kiss I've ever had.

"No, it wasn't." Trevor leans toward me again, brushing my hair from my face. "You're the one that got away, Mandy."

I'm glad the car isn't in motion, because I'm pretty certain I'd swerve into oncoming traffic about now. All I can do is stare at him. The look in Trevor's eyes is earnest, not like he's teasing me. Is this really happening? Is something with Trevor even remotely possible? But of course not, it's not like he lives here, and my life will be once it's February and I can finally leave my job and move home.

Trevor pulls back, as much as his muscle-bound body can in my small car. "Can you say something? Am I out of line?"

"No," I say, once I can actually speak again. "It's just...you know. I'd thought we'd have a bit of fun," I say, inwardly wincing at the white lie, but scared to admit that I've been hoping for more, "and that we'd go back to our normal lives in a few days. You've just made it serious."

"Mandy, I *am* serious." Trevor reaches out and puts his hand on mine.

I flinch, not believing what he's saying. I'm famously bad at choosing men to date, so it's hard to believe it would be any different with Trevor. Trevor Collins! We strung each other along in high school and I can't believe that he's not doing the same thing now. Sure, everything *feels* different, but I can't believe that it *is* different.

"I... I don't know." Trevor looks serious, but... Can I really believe him? "I need to get these groceries home and in the refrigerator. I'll drop you off on the way home."

Out of the corner of my eye, I see Trevor nod and slump back in his seat.

I grip the steering wheel tightly, wishing I could go back to the touch football game and take back tackling Trevor. All of this started because of that and I didn't even mean to do it.

~

"WHEN WILL I EVER LEARN?" I hate the whine in my voice, but I can't help it.

"I don't know…" Grace says, leaning back in her chair, her hands wrapped around a grande hot chocolate.

"I mean, he looked serious. That kiss was *definitely* serious. But… come *on*. After all this time? The guy who got away is actually interested in me? A *pro football player* is interested in me? That doesn't happen to girls like me!"

My voice goes shrill and I slap my hand over my mouth when I see people at the next table looking over at us. It's not like I need my problems need to be broadcast.

"You're not going to like this, but I'm still going to say it, Mandy. You need to talk to Trevor," Grace says, seriously. "You two have been circling each other since high school. I don't know how you think you could just hook up with him for a night, maybe two, and have that be it."

"But…"

"Mandy, look at me. There are no buts about it. There are too many emotions and too much history between you two."

I slump in my seat, briefly cursing the Christmas music. *All I Want for Christmas Is You* comes on and all I want for Christmas is to hide from the world or at least live in a universe where I didn't feel bad for being single. I want Trevor so bad, but I know it would never work. If we didn't figure things out in high school, how can I expect that we could work things out *now*?

"I don't know..."

"Mandy, I know and I know you do, too. I know it's scary, but you have to face it. You'll never know, otherwise."

"But what if everything goes south, like with every other guy I've liked or dated? Why should I believe Trevor is any different?"

"Relationships are mysterious. The thing is, you don't and can't know. You just have to take the chance and put your heart out there."

"I know, I know. It's just my heart is bruised, you know? I don't have faith in myself." I look away from Grace, unable to meet her eyes. There are tears pricking at my eyes and I know that if I see sympathy from Grace, it will push me over the edge.

"Oh, sweetie. You're an amazing woman. You're smart and talented and beautiful. Any man that doesn't recognize that is an abject fool."

I smile at Grace and wipe tears from the corners of my eyes. "You're making me cry."

"I'm ready to cry if you're going to give up. Don't give up."

"I'll try." I take a deep breath, trying to calm my emotions. If there's one thing the holidays are good for, it's an abundance of emotions.

"One last thing. Despite how Trevor was in high school, he is not an abject fool."

CHAPTER 8

TREVOR

*R*eginald, bro. I'm sorry, but I'm out. I've already talked to Coach Freeman. I don't want to be crippled for life – and if I keep playing, my knee is going to go out and that's exactly what's going to happen. It's not public yet, but I'm retiring. It's not a publicity stunt, not like Josiah pulled two years ago."

"Man… We need our captain back. You're the glue that holds us together. We're getting our asses handed to us. Even the Royals beat us this year." I can hear the frustration and disappointment in my former teammate's voice. The Austin Blues have been hurting this year, since our old coach packed up and went to another team.

"I'm sorry you guys have it rough this year, really. But I'm not kidding about retiring."

Reginald's laugh is sharp and fast. "You seriously think you're going to be happy with life in a small town? I can keep the door open a little while longer, but don't wait too long…"

"You know the flashy lifestyle was never really for me. Not saying it's not fun and seductive, but it's not a long-term thing for me. Coaching high school football is where my future is – my school was great when I was there and I want to take them to state again, this time as their coach. I want to give back to the school that gave me my start."

"You're a better man than I am, Trevor. Look, I gotta run. Esme's nearly here and we have to bust ass to get out to her mom's."

"Yeah, I gotta jet, too. I got a Christmas ham to bake."

"Dude. You're *cooking*? What's her name?"

I smile as I think of Mandy. It's useless to pretend I don't love my best friend's sister.

"Mandy. And it's for her brother, too. Idiot dislocated his shoulder. I'm just the fill-in cook."

"Don't try to downplay it. I know how you are about cooking – you don't just do that for anyone. You only cook for family. They must be important."

"True. I'm known Mandy and Jimmy since I was six."

Reginald's deep voice booms in laughter, and then he lets out a long, low whistle.

"This is the girl that got away, isn't it? Don't think I've forgotten you mentioning her."

"Yeah, that's her. Not sure how it's going, because everything stops before it starts or she's mad at me."

"The madder she is, the more she cares. Look at me and Esme."

I laugh. Reginald's wife is a spitfire. At barely five feet, she has Reginald and all two-hundred-sixty pounds of his muscle under control. Reginald may be one of the superstars of the Austin Blues, but she leads their marriage.

"Yeah, something tells me Mandy and Esme would get on like a house on fire."

A car horn bleats three times and I can hear Reginald huffing as he walks through the winter air.

"Look. You figure it out. You've won three Superbowl rings – you can figure out the plays for this girl. I'll bet my ring on it."

I sure hope so. I'm ready to bet everything on Mandy.

"As much as you may think I'm a dumb jock, let me show you what I can do in the kitchen."

I turn and smile at Mandy, but she's leaning against the back door, arms across her deliciously plump chest, her eyebrow raised at me.

"I don't know how you think you can cook better than I can," she finally says, going to the sink and washing her hands, then pushing up her sleeves. My eyes lock on her full breasts and how they shift under the thin fabric of her blouse as she pulls her hair up into a bun.

"Mandy, you know I adore you," I raise my eyes and focus on her brilliant blue eyes. "But you can't cook and we know it. Everyone knows it."

Mandy's cheeks color, but she doesn't look away.

"Doesn't mean I can't learn." Her voice is defensive, but she's not retreating. *Good*. I can work with this. I love that she's willing to try and learn, instead of doubling down in stubbornness.

"I'm glad to hear that. What we're going to do isn't too complicated, not like French cooking, but we do have to get it right."

"Uh huh."

I watch her eyes rake up and down my body, lingering over the apron I've wrapped around my waist. "Do you want an apron? It'll protect that pretty blouse of yours." Though if she got something on her blouse and I had to take it off…

Mandy makes short work of chopping the vegetables I stack in front of her. The carrot matchsticks are a little uneven, but it doesn't matter at all.

Wiping my hands on my apron, I go to the fridge and pull out some potatoes.

"Okay. These need to be peeled and then sliced into rounds. Sound good?"

"Sure."

I slice up several onions, then turn my attention back to Mandy. She's focused on the potatoes and she's doing an excellent job. My guess is that she's just never cooked much, not that she has no skill for cooking.

"All done," she says, looking up at me, a smile on her face.

"Those are perfect." This is not a lie. The more she helps me, the more I see her relaxing and looking confident. "Now let's trim up some more of the vegetables, and then—"

Mandy's forehead creases as she interrupts me. "What's with all the vegetables? Was buying meat a diversion? Are you secretly a *vegetarian?*"

"Oh, Mandy. Honey. No." I laugh loudly, wiping my eyes and then instantly regretting it as tears stream from my eyes, thanks to onion juice I forgot to wash from my hands.

"I didn't think it was that funny."

I squint at Mandy and I can see she's closing in on herself again.

"I'm sorry. I didn't mean to make you uncomfortable. I couldn't maintain this," I say, gesturing down toward my body, puffing out my chest a little when Mandy's eyes follow my hands and linger on my body, "if I didn't eat meat. You'd be hard-pressed to find a vegetarian football player – one, the guys just aren't like that; and two, it would be too hard to get all the protein we need."

"Thanks." Mandy's smile is thin, but at least she's still here. "I suppose I see what you're saying."

"Alright. Let's get everything ready for the salad, and then we should be good to go. The rest we can take care of in the morning."

I move to where Mandy is at the counter and stand beside her, and we both start chopping. I have her chopping bread into squares, to bake into croutons.

God. This is what I want, right here. Mandy and I, side by side, working and living and loving together.

A familiar twitch and tightening hits my groin and I cough.

"That's it for now. Beer?"

"That sounds amazing. Yes, please."

I grab two beers from the fridge, then we head into the living room. For once, I'm glad that Jimmy isn't here, but upstairs resting.

"What was this talk of you moving home?" I ask as I watch Mandy settle onto the opposite end of the couch. A primal instinct has me wanting to reach out and pull her close to me, but I know that would be the wrong move with her.

Mandy sighs and peels the edge of the label on the beer bottle she's holding.

"It's been tough in Seattle. I miss my friends here and I miss my brother. It's going to sound quaint, so don't laugh," she says, giving me a long, narrow-eyed look of warning, "but I miss life in a smaller town. I want a family of my own and I'm not sure I want to do that in Seattle. I don't want to have to worry about my kids going outside to play."

"I know what you mean," I say, taking a long drink of my beer. "I've wanted to move home for a long time, too."

Mandy's laugh is full and rich, and it makes me want to make her laugh every hour of every day.

"Yeah, right. You're just trying to charm me again. I don't believe a word of it." The smile Mandy gives me, full of play-fulness and affection, it goes straight to my heart. "Who would give up the career that you fought so hard for? I remember how you worked your ass off in high school. Playing pro ball isn't something someone just gives up."

"Maybe I am trying to charm you…" I say, ignoring the fact that she's wrong. I'm leaving the Blues and coming home. I move closer to her on the couch and smile when she shivers as I run my fingers down her arm. "Maybe I'm trying to match your flirting game."

"What flirting game?" Mandy asks, her voice suddenly quieter and breathless.

I move my hand across her wrist and take her hand in mine, pulling her closer to me. She doesn't resist.

"The flirting game of tackling me the other day." She's now so close I can feel her breath puffing against my mouth. My mouth presses against her plump lips and her body presses against mine, her hand tentatively wrapping around my neck. Kissing her again is fan-fucking-tastic. Teasing her, I pull back from our kiss. "The flirting game that you started in middle school." I kiss her again, my tongue teasing her. The taste of beer lingers on her lips and it's indescribable how good she tastes and how much I want to drink Mandy and her kiss in.

"I'm not...sure..." Mandy blinks her eyes rapidly, her fingers pushing up into my hair. "I'm pretty sure it was you who teased me back then."

"Are you sure about that?" I lower my mouth to her neck and scrape her skin with my teeth, before sucking at her neck and making her moan.

"Oh my... And what... what about the mistletoe?" Mandy groans and I can feel her body heat burning against my body.

"What about," I lick her neck slowly, "the mistletoe?" I kiss her along her jaw and she leans into me. I drop a hand down to her chest and slowly caress her breasts, and discover her nipples poking urgently against my fingertips.

"That...was you...teasing...me."

I snake my arm around her waist and urge her even closer. Mandy moves so that she's straddling my lap and every fiber of my being is loudly demanding to strip off her clothes and make love to her all night long. Tonight, and every night to come.

Mandy's blue eyes meet mine, then she cups her soft hands along my jaw and lowers her mouth to mine. She nips at my lips, then parts my lips with her tongue, and then I'm falling into her and falling into how good she feels, how right Mandy feels. My hands roam her body, loving the feel of her soft curves, the weight of her on top of me.

Wrapping my hands around her ass, I bless whomever made leggings, because I can feel her ass clearly and I'm already fantasizing about bending her over and losing myself inside of her. If just kissing and groping her feels like this, burying my cock deep inside of Mandy is going to make me lose my mind in the best possible way.

"I think we need," Mandy nips at my earlobe, "go somewhere more—"

We both freeze as heavy footsteps echo as Jimmy walks down the stairs from his bedroom. In a scene that feels like it's out of a high school playbook, Mandy leaps off my lap and frantically smooths her hair and clothes, looking around wildly like her parents are about to walk in and discover us. I try and hide the raging hard-on pressing against my jeans, quickly grabbing a throw blanket to spread across my lap.

Like that is going to fool anyone, especially Jimmy...

Jimmy turns the corner from the stairs and looks at us, one arm in a sling and the other hand wiping his face.

"Man, I didn't expect to sleep so long. What've you two been up to?"

CHAPTER 9

MANDY

heers!" Jimmy, Grace, Trevor, and I all clink glasses once everyone has loaded up their plates with the meal Trevor and I cooked today. For as much as I *don't* know about cooking, I have to admit I had fun with Trevor in the kitchen. He made everything seem interesting and not-intimidating. It made me want to spend more time in the kitchen and learn how to cook better.

With his fork halfway to his mouth, Jimmy looks from Trevor to me, then back to Trevor.

"Trevor, I think we all need to know – what did you cook and what did Mandy cook?" His eyes glitter with laughter.

"Hey! I resent that!" I exclaim, though I'm laughing. I load up my fork with scalloped potatoes and I groan with genuine pleasure when I taste it.

"Well, I guess we know what dish Mandy made," Jimmy says, eyeing the scalloped potatoes warily.

"It was entirely a joint effort," Trevor says, a megawatt smile on his lips. "Mandy was a joy to cook with. I don't know why you all don't think she can cook."

Grace coughs, then stares at Jimmy, her eyes open.

"Trevor? Is there rum in the eggnog you've been drinking? Haven't you heard about Mandy's cooking? I know you two haven't seen each other in a while, but… Mandy is kind of legendary."

"You guys," I groan, rolling my eyes. "I'm not that bad!"

"Yes, you are!" Jimmy and Grace chime in unison.

"Well, be that as it may," Trevor says, pausing to take a bite of food. "I did lead the cooking, yes. That doesn't mean Mandy couldn't hold her own in the kitchen. And everything truly was a joint effort."

"You'll never get a husband if you can't cook," Jimmy teases, taking the joke too far.

"Or maybe I just need a husband who cooks. Who says it's still the woman's role to do all the cooking?" I try to keep my voice light and do my damnedest to keep my emotions in check, but my brother's dig hurts – and he knows it.

"Oh, come on!" I slap the counter of the bar and shake my head in disbelief as I watch the game on the big screen TV. I take a long drink of my beer and cover my mouth at the burp that rises up. "How did the ref miss that interference?"

The other guys at the bar and the bartender all look at me and nod sadly. The refs this game have it in for us. This isn't their first bad call.

"They're sure making it hard for us to get to post-season," the guy on my left says.

"Oh, don't be so hasty. That wasn't an interference and the call was good."

I swear under my breath at the voice coming from my right, even before I turn and see his face.

"What are you doing here?" I turn and ask Trevor. I'm still upset about what happened at dinner, even if it wasn't his fault. I left because I needed space, not to be tracked down.

"Looking for you, as it happens. You left rather abruptly, you might remember."

I grab my beer tightly and look away from Trevor. As soon as dinner was over, I excused myself to come out for a beer, alone. I thought I'd been graceful about it, but maybe not.

"It's just...the holidays are hard. I hate that the first question everyone asks is if I have a boyfriend or a fiancé. And yes, I get that my cooking skills are...rudimentary, but maybe people could let up a bit." I admit, hearing the tightness in my voice. A couple of beers hasn't been enough to help me relax. Right now, I'm just down on the holidays. No boyfriend. Mad at my brother. "I'm going to head home tomorrow."

"Do you have to go back to work so soon?"

"Not really, no," I say, waving to the bartender for another beer. I hold two fingers up. Might as well get one for Trevor, since he doesn't look like he's just passing through. "It's just...I had a bad breakup recently. I was hoping to escape that over the holidays. That's all."

"I understand," Trevor says, quickly moving onto the newly empty barstool beside me.

"You have got to be kidding, right? You must have more girl-friends than you can even manage." The words come out of my mouth sour and jealous, and I immediately regret it. "Sorry," I add quickly. "It's just…hard night and big feelings."

Trevor gives me a long look, then takes a long drink of his beer.

"Anyway," I say, wrapping my fingers around my beer bottle to stop them from shaking. What was I thinking, admitting this to Trevor? "Anyway, did Jimmy send you here to be all cagey, to lure me back to the house?" I ask, keeping Trevor in my line of sight as I watch the game. We're halfway through the third quarter, ball in hand and we're in the middle of a big drive. A touchdown is looking imminent.

"No," he says, a slow smile spreading across his mouth. "I came for you. Me. The only agenda is mine."

My insides flutter and somersault as I listen to Trevor. Our unfinished business washes over me and before I even realize what I'm doing, my fingers are on his wrist and stroking that spot where the base of his thumb meets his wrist.

"That's a dangerous thing you're doing there," Trevor says, but he doesn't pull away. The rest of the bar cheers as our team makes a touchdown, but Trevor and I keep staring at each other, the electricity building up all over again.

"Maybe a girl needs a little danger in her life? Why don't we just have some fun. You're leaving soon and I'm—"

"Hold up," Trevor says, putting a finger on my lips. "I'm actually not leaving. I'm back to stay."

I blink rapidly, wrapping my mind around the words I'm pretty sure he just said. I haven't had so much beer that I'm hallucinating, have I?

"I… What?"

"I've been offered a job coaching at the high school. Coach Fitzgerald is retiring in June." Trevor pauses, not once looking away from me. "I've already accepted the job. We're both coming back home, Mandy."

"Oh," I mumble, unable to say anything coherent.

The universe has a funny way of doing things. I thought coming home would give me a break from the heartache I've felt, but now? Now I'm going to see Trevor regularly? That makes my heart ache in a different, more painful way. I honestly don't know if I can take seeing him around, eventually settling down with another woman. It would feel like just another man that I've loved, but who didn't love me back.

"Mandy, why do you look so blue? I thought you would be happy to hear this," Trevor says, leaning closer to me. "Jimmy telling me that you were moving home is the reason I agreed to the job."

CHAPTER 10

TREVOR

*E*xcuse me, what?" Mandy's head snaps toward me, her eyes blazing.

"When I heard that you're moving back here," I say, reaching out and putting my hand over hers, "that sealed the deal for me. Coach Fitzgerald has been after me to take his job for months now. When he heard I was retiring, he started campaigning to get me to take over."

"But…" Mandy's mouth open and closes. Her eyes are bright and I can see her mind racing, even though her mouth keeps opening and closing, and no words come out. "Would you really be happy here?"

"Why wouldn't I be happy here? Everything I need to make me happy is here. *You're* here." I squeeze her hands with mine and gently caress them. Her body tenses a little bit, but she doesn't pull her hands away.

"Won't you miss playing with your team? Going from professional sports to be a high school coach, that's a really big change. What about the fame and flashy lifestyle?"

"Of course I'll miss playing with the team. They've become my brothers. We're a family. They mean the world to me, but pro ball isn't the life I want. My knee can't take much more damage, anyway. Worrying about hurting it keeps me from playing like I want to play and how my team needs me to play."

Mandy's eyes narrow and I get the distinct sense that she doesn't believe me about any of this.

"But is it going to be enough, to be back here?"

"Mandy," I say, pulling her hands so that she's standing in front of me, between my legs. "Look, sure. Fame is fun. But it gets old. Believe me when I say it's not a line that I want to settle down, too." I look into Mandy's eyes and her body stills. "It's why I'm moving back home. You were the one who got away. Now's my chance to fix that."

I stand up and wrap my arms around Mandy, pulling her into a kiss. I have every intention of going slow, enjoy this moment…but when she wraps her arms around me and pulls me tightly against her soft curves, I can't help myself. My tongue pushes hard at her lips, desperate to taste her again. She needs a reason to believe I'm staying and I want my kiss to show her just how serious I am.

Mandy moans into my mouth and deepens our kiss, and I pull her closer, desperate for there to be no space between us.

A loud ruckus around us catches my attention and we both pull apart, panting as we stare into each other's eyes.

"Did we score?" Mandy asks, glancing toward the TV above the bar. But all that's on is a beer commercial.

"I think so." I don't give a fuck about the game on the TV. All I care about is Mandy and doing what we've needed to do for years. I let my fingers caress her waist, my heart pounding that this is finally happening. "I don't care, Mandy. I care about you. Let's get out of here."

CHAPTER 11

MANDY

*T*revor and I practically fall over ourselves as we leave the bar. The air has changed between us. The flirting we did during the football game, that pales compared to the electricity between us now. This attraction, it's not about having fun – there's nothing casual about the way we're looking at each other or talking to each other. Everything contains the gravity of commitment.

"I always wanted you. Fuck. I wanted you so bad in high school, but your brother would have massacred me."

I grin at Trevor and squeezes his hand tighter in mine. The pent-up desire I've had for Trevor unlocks within me and fills the very essence of my being.

"I wanted you, too, but you were too popular. My brother warned me about you, anyway. He said you were no good and that you'd break my heart."

Trevor's laugh echoes down the streets and a dog barks in the distance.

"That sure sounds like Jimmy. But to be fair, he was probably right. I didn't know what I was doing back then and I probably *would* have broken your heart. Even though I've dreamed about you for so long, I'm glad that this is happening now. I'm not scared of what I want. I'm the man I've always wanted to be."

"Are you sure?" I ask, needing reassurance. I'm happier than I've ever been, but there's a little voice inside my head that's telling me it's not going to work out. It's never worked out with other guys before, so why should I think it will now?

But this is Trevor. I know Trevor and he knows me. This isn't just some random flirtation.

Trevor stops walking and holds me so that I stop walking, too.

"Mandy," his voice quiets as he pulls me closer to him. "You are the one I've always wanted, too. It's never worked out with anybody else, because they weren't you."

"I think that's why it's never worked out for me, with anyone else, either," I whisper, pressing my body against Trevor's. "This is just scary, you know? I've dreamed about you for so long, too, that it almost doesn't seem real that this is really happening. I want it to happen and I truly love you."

"Then let me show you how much I love you, too." Trevor pushes my hair back from my face and holds my jaw gently as he lowers his mouth to mine, then gives me the slowest and most intimate kiss ever.

Our tongues dance slowly as we stand on the sidewalk. An urgency grows in our kiss, but it's not the raw urgency of lust, but an urgency to do what we wanted to do for so long to seal our love for each other.

"Oh my God! It's about time you two hooked up!" Grace's voice calls from across the street.

Trevor and I bump heads as I jump at the sound of Grace's voice.

Trevor hugs me tightly and we see her crossing the deserted, snowy street to meet us. Snow is starting to fall again and I'm grinning like an idiot.

"I'm working on a long-term arrangement," Trevor calls out, tightening his arms around me. My insides quiver with nerves and excitement. I can't believe this is really happening.

Grace narrows her eyes at Trevor when she finally makes it over to us.

"Trevor Collins," she says, her voice stern. "If you string my best friend along, you will have *me* to answer to," she pokes Trevor in the chest and glares at him, "and I will make your life miserable. Are we clear?"

"Yes, ma'am," he says, smiling. "I want nothing but to make her happy. You're a fierce friend. I respect that."

"Good. You okay?" She turns to me and her face softens. "I'm really happy for you. No one deserves happiness more than you do."

"Tonight's turning out alright," I say, laughing and holding Trevor's body tightly. His body is so strong and so warm, and I can't wait to be somewhere private with him so that we can make love. Finally.

"Good! I'm really happy for both of you."

"This is better than winning a Super Bowl ring. Now if you'll excuse us, I need to take Mandy home."

My stomach flip flops with anticipation and happiness. Grace leans in and gives me a quick hug, and then Trevor and I make our way to his hotel.

～

"Do you need anything else?" The hotel clerk says, batting her long eyelashes at Trevor. I don't even mind that she's ignoring that I exist because I know the Trevor is mine.

"No, just a full breakfast in the morning. We've got all we need in each other," he says smiling, his eyes never leaving mine. "We're never going to be apart, ever again."

I giggle as we go up in the elevator at the biggest hotel in the city. This feels like we're teenagers sneaking off to do what we can't do at our parents' homes.

"I think she wanted an autograph," I tease, pushing my hand inside Trevor's coat, feeling his warm body under my fingertips. He flexes his muscles and I gasp at how strong his body is.

"She could have had an autograph if she asked. But that's all that she, or any other woman, can ever have. No one will ever be able to take me away from you."

We rush through the hallway, then fumble with the keycard for the door. When it finally clicks, we're through the door in a flash, pushing it closed behind us.

"Finally. Alone." We both shrug off our coats and let them fall straight to the floor. We rush toward the bed, shedding our clothes as we go.

As I stand, nearly naked in front of Trevor, I feel comfortable in my skin for the first time.

"You are so stunning," he says, his mouth opens as his eyes roam over my body. He caresses my skin and it sends shock-waves through my body. His touch is so reverential and it's so different than how I've felt with other guys. Trevor makes me feel beautiful and desirable.

"You're pretty nice yourself." I smile at him, biting my lip as I look at his muscular body. Years of football has left him more ripped than I thought someone could actually be. I see the scar by his knee and I feel a pang at the loss he's had, but I also feel joy that he's back here now and with me.

"Only pretty nice?" His voice is mock-hurt and it makes me giggle.

"Okay, maybe *very* nice."

"Hmpf."

"Though perhaps I could upgrade my assessment after a bit more...investigation." I let my fingers dance over his skin and reach down to feel his shaft. He's hard and long, and his cock feels glorious.

"Investigation," he says, his voice deepening. "I support investigation."

I shudder as his fingers find my wetness and teases at my clit, massaging it so lightly that flames of desire burn through my body. He wraps his other arm around my waist, holding me close as we stroke and tease each other.

"I want to taste you," he says, and my core flutters at the idea of him between my legs. I bite my lip and nod my head at him, and he walks us over to the bed and gently pushes me down on it. He grabs a pillow and holds it next to my hips. "Put this under your hips."

I lift my hips and he slides the pillow underneath me, and I tremble from how exposed I am to him right now. Trevor stares at my core, a big smile on his lips and his eyes bright with excitement – he looks like a kid ready to devour a birthday cake.

Trevor kneels in front of me, my body shivering as each caress from his tongue moves up my legs and closer to my hot center. When his tongue slides into my wetness, I moan from how exquisite it feels. His tongue circles around my clit, driving me crazy and aching for more.

I've never felt anything so good as this and my body quickly starts tensing and trembling, as I feel an orgasm rapidly building inside my body. I've wanted Trevor for so long and this all feels like the most delicious dream. My senses are on overdrive, as my emotions push me rapidly to a point of explosion.

"Oh!" I cry out as an orgasm suddenly surges through my body, filling me with pleasure as I look down at Trevor. He stares up into my eyes, holding me tightly and slowing his licking, drawing my orgasm out so that I enjoy it longer.

"You taste so good," he says, reaching up to play with one of my breasts as he moves so that his fit body is balanced over mine.

"That was amazing. Your body is so gorgeous," I say, my hands squeezing at the muscles in his arms.

Trevor grins and flexes his muscles over me, and it just makes something in me go weak. This man has the body of a museum statue...and he likes me. No, he *loves* me. I lift my head up to Trevor and kiss him deeply. Tasting myself on his tongue makes me squirm with lust.

"Your body is gorgeous, Mandy. You're the most beautiful woman I've ever seen."

I close my eyes in pleasure as his cock pushes into me and I instantly know that we are a perfect match. His lips claim my mouth in another kiss and our bodies begin rocking together, our rhythm moving faster and faster.

"Damn, you feel so good!" When I look up at Trevor, his eyes are filled with awe as he looks at me. He thrusts deeper and faster into me, and I feel another orgasm building up inside of me.

As Trevor moves faster and faster, I spread my legs farther and push my hips up to him, inviting him to plunge deeper inside of me. His big cock fills me perfectly and I wiggle my hips in joy as he thrusts against my g-spot over and over.

"I'm not going to last much longer," I moan, wrapping my arms around him and holding him tightly.

"Me, neither." Trevor begins thrusting faster and it takes my breath away. Each thrust hits all of my nerve endings in just the right way and then my orgasm is so close and I hear myself crying out and bucking my body against his, desperately aching for release.

"Oh, Trevor! I love you so much!" I moan his name over and over as my second orgasm crashes over me.

"I love...you!" Trevor thrusts deep inside of me and stays there as his body shakes and he groans in pleasure.

My body shaking, I hold Trevor tightly to me. He collapses at my side and then immediately wraps his arms around me and holds me in a fierce bearhug. I snuggle into his embrace, my head against his chest hears his rapidly beating heart begin to slow down as he catches his breath. For the first time in I don't know how long, I feel loved and like I know where I fit in the world. I fit with Trevor.

"I think I'm going to like moving back home." I smile as I look up into Trevor's eyes. This moment feels more perfect than any moment I've ever experienced. I feel wanted and loved. Being with Trevor feels like home.

"If there's anything I can do to help you stay even longer…" There's a wicked smile on Trevor's lips and it sends me into a fit of giggles.

"Your love is enough to make me follow you anywhere, Trevor. I know, now, why it never worked out with anybody else. It's because they weren't you."

The look on Trevor's face softens and his lips find mine and he kisses me slowly. It feels magical to know that I've finally found my one true love.

"It's the same for me, too. I always knew it was you, but I was so scared of your brother."

I roll over so that I'm straddling Trevor's muscular body and I wiggle my hips.

"And I think we need to make up for lost time. Don't you?"

"Absolutely! I'm never letting you get away, ever again."

EPILOGUE — MANDY & TREVOR

No cheating!" Jimmy hollers at me across the field as he sees me looking at Trevor. Of course I'm going to pass the ball to my boyfriend—he's the best player out here!

"But we're on the same team!" I yell back at my brother. He rolls his eyes and turns away for a split second and I throw the ball.

"Of course she did!" Grace shouts as she chases after Trevor.

"I'm king of the field!" Trevor does an end zone dance and, for the millionth time in the past year, my heart explodes with love and happiness. I run down the field to join him, throwing my arms around him and covering his face in kisses.

"We are the best team ever."

"Anything for my Mandy," he says, then pulls me in to a deep kiss.

"Dude! How many times I have to tell you to keep your hands off my sister?" Jimmy starts running towards us, laughing

151

and with his fists up in the air. Trevor wraps his arms around me even tighter, with a look of amused defiance on his face.

Despite Trevor and I practically living together these days, Jimmy still does that protective older brother thing, though now it's just a running joke among all of us. It's been clear since last Christmas that Trevor and I belong to each other and that nothing can stand between us.

"I'm never letting Mandy go and you know that, Jimmy." Trevor laughs, but there's still a hint of impatience to his voice, which makes me realize he's about as tired of Jimmy's joking as I am.

"Trevor." There's an edge to Jimmy's voice that confuses me. It's like he's serious all of a sudden, but I have no idea why.

"Is everything okay between you two?" I ask, turning to Trevor. I snuggle into his arms and hold him tightly. If Jimmy has a beef with Trevor, he's going to have to go through me too.

Trevor looks me and nods.

"Can we get the game moving?" Grace calls out, crossing her arms over her chest and shivering a little bit. "It'll be dark soon and we need to get dinner going."

"Okay, okay."

We play the second half of touch football, and I laugh every time Trevor intentionally trips so that Grace or Jimmy can score a touchdown.

Trevor throws the ball to me and I sprint as fast as I can down the field. Jimmy reaches out for my flag, but misses and I scream as I keep running.

"I made it! I get the final touchdown!"

I spike the ball on the cold ground and dance around it, waving my arms in the air.

I start to walk away, but I catch the look on Grace's face and it stills me. She makes a little motion with her hand for me to turn around, and I do. Trevor is kneeling on the ground, his hand outstretched to me.

"Is this... Are you..." I can't even say the words because so much emotion is rolling over me. I walk over to Trevor and place my hand in his. One million thoughts explode in my mind all at once.

"Mandy. When you tackled me last year, it gave me so much hope that what I always wanted was what you wanted, too. Ever since then, and especially since last Christmas, you have brought me more joy and love than I ever thought I would be lucky enough to find. You are an incredible woman and I want you on my team forever. Just you and me, tackling the world." Trevor's brown eyes fill with tears and his voice trembles, and it spikes into my heart so much that I start crying, too. "Mandy, my best cheerleader, will you marry me?"

It takes me a few seconds to do more than simultaneously laugh and cry, but I finally get it together.

"Yes!"

Trevor smiles so wide that I think his cheeks are going to split open. My eyes never leave him as he reaches into the inside pocket of his puffy jacket and pulls out a dark velvet box. His strong fingers fumble as he opens it, revealing the prettiest diamond ring I've ever seen. The setting sun hits the ring and it dances with color. Trevor gently takes my hand and slides the ring on, then I tackle him and kiss him passionately.

"I love you more than life itself," I tell Trevor, not wanting to let him go.

"Good grief! Get a room!" Grace calls out, laughter in her voice.

Trevor and I get to our feet, never once taking our hands off each other. We walk over to join Grace and Jimmy, and I look at Jimmy, not knowing what to expect.

"You treat her right, you hear?"

"You know, I'm standing right here, brother." I roll my eyes and squeeze Trevor tighter.

"Show me the ring!" Grace squeals and I turn to her, smiling so much my cheeks hurt.

Trevor gives me a quick kiss and chuckles, then lightly pushes me toward Grace. She oohs and aahs over the ring, giving me so many hugs I can barely breathe.

"You're next, you know," I tease.

"You're not wrong... I've been dating someone I really like. I think there's potential."

"Whoa. That's something, coming from you. Is this why I haven't seen you as much lately? I've been wondering what you were up to."

"Yeah," she says, looking away and blushing a little. "I've invited him to watch the game after Christmas dinner this year."

"Yay! I can't wait to meet him!" I give Grace a huge hug and cross my fingers that she really has found the guy for her. I know she wants a family just as much as I do and I'd love it if we had children at the same time.

"Come on, you two! It's cold out here. Let's get dinner and to celebrating!"

$\approx$

"I love your brother and Grace, but I'm glad we're finally alone." Trevor pulls me close as we walk into his house. For the first time since he proposed, my mind quiets, because there's a new peace in my world. He gives me a slow kiss and my love for him expands even more.

"Me, too. I've wanted to be alone with you since the game." I push my body against Trevor's and run my hand under his sweater and across his smooth, hot skin.

We nearly fall over each other's feet as we rush to his bedroom, removing each other's clothes as we go, giggling at our shared clumsiness and urgency to be naked.

Trevor turns on the light to watch me finish undressing. It took a long time for me to be comfortable with this, but he loves me – every inch of me – and has always been incredibly vocal about how much he loves my curvy body.

"You never need to hide anything from me. You're the most beautiful woman in the world."

"I love you, Trevor."

"I love you, too, Mandy." He pulls me into a kiss, then playfully pushes me onto the bed and moves his strong, muscular body over mine. "Now, do you think we need to get a new mattress set?"

"Hm..." I moan as his mouth and hot tongue find that tender spot on my neck. Spreading my legs for Trevor and pushing my hips up to him, I cry out as he pushes into me. "I think that calls for investigation. Let's see how much this bed can handle, and then ask me later."

"Deal."

Our bodies move together, hot and sweaty, and I know – this is just the beginning of our forever.

Thank you so much for reading *"Santa Loves Curves"*! If you enjoyed this book, please consider leaving a review or rating on your favorite retailer, Bookbub, or Goodreads! Thank you!!

Sign up for my mailing list!
http://eepurl.com/dh59Xr
Subscribers receive updates on new books, plus exclusive bonus content!

For a full listing of my books, please visit:

https://www.loveheartbooks.com

Ingram Content Group UK Ltd.
Milton Keynes UK
UKHW021831170323
418736UK00016B/891

9 798215 328408